About the Author

Donald McCrory took early retirement from his post as Head of Hispanic and Germanic Studies at the American Intl University in London to focus on 1) creative writing, 2) yoga and 3) on further study of oriental languages (Sanskrit, Hindi and Mandarin) as well as on Eastern philosophies (Advaita Vedanta and Buddhism, in particular).

His published works include historical biographies, several academic essays and articles, four novels, and he has won several prizes for his poetry. Until retirement, he was a Fellow of the Royal Society of Geography. He currently lives in Spain.

Noah's Noble Mission

Donald McCrory

Noah's Noble Mission

Olympia Publishers
London

www.olympiapublishers.com
OLYMPIA PAPERBACK EDITION

Copyright © Donald McCrory 2024

The right of Donald McCrory to be identified as author of
this work has been asserted in accordance with sections 77 and 78 of
the Copyright, Designs and Patents Act 1988.

All Rights Reserved

No reproduction, copy or transmission of this publication
may be made without written permission.
No paragraph of this publication may be reproduced,
copied or transmitted save with the written permission of the publisher,
or in accordance with the provisions
of the Copyright Act 1956 (as amended).

Any person who commits any unauthorised act in relation to
this publication may be liable to criminal
prosecution and civil claims for damage.

A CIP catalogue record for this title is
available from the British Library.

ISBN: 978-1-80439-485-4

This is a work of fiction.
Names, characters, places and incidents originate from the writer's
imagination. Any resemblance to actual persons, living or dead, is
purely coincidental.

First Published in 2024

Olympia Publishers
Tallis House
2 Tallis Street
London
EC4Y 0AB

Printed in Great Britain

Dedication

I dedicate this book to all my teachers and students, in particular to Mr Leon Maclaren, former leader of the School of Economic Science in London. I am equally indebted to Benjamin Crème, former editor of *Share Intl* and spokesperson for Maitreya and for news of The Second Coming.

Mention must be made of Richard Gombrich and of Bhikku Bodhi whose studies of Buddhism have transformed my thinking.

I also have to mention my niece Annette McCrory, Julie Perigot and her husband Dan Dumitrescu – now residing in Barcelona – Antonio Fernandez Luna de Pont, who has become my mentor in all things to do with modern Spanish usage and with everyday life in today´s Spain, Elena Airini Alexandru and to Colin Clark – who lives in Chorley in Lancashire and as far as I know, is the only person who has read all of my published work to date and is also.... cover. All are enlightened beings and have become my very best of friends over several years.

Acknowledgements

I would like to acknowledge the SES (School of Economic Science) in London, the Buddhist Society in London, the SOM (School of Meditation) in London, White Eagle Lodge in Liphook in Hampshire – that offers courses in Astrology and Healing – and the BWY (British Wheel of Yoga) in the UK of which I was a practising teacher for many years.

CHAPTER 1

No one disagreed; every tongue that wagged in mid-Wales said the same thing about retired maths teacher Noah Salmon who, one day and seemingly on a whim, chose to spend what remained of his retirement years in a small town near the Brecon Beacons. Very few men, single and in their seventies, suddenly up-stick and move to what his former friends called the 'middle of nowhere'. Yet that is exactly what Noah did. 'But why mid-Wales?', 'Why near Brecon Beacons? and 'Why us?' the locals asked themselves, and very much wanted to ask him but no one had been able to and that's because he was rarely seen.

Noah, since his sudden emergence from no one knew where, had become a recluse (some locals soon claimed he should have joined a hermitage) and was to be seen only on his early morning walks. But very few saw him because most of the locals, especially those of his venerable age, got up much later; very occasionally, he could be seen on a Wednesday morning, market day, but only if you were second in the queue because he would be the first. Yes, he was a 'will-o'-the-wisp' figure, a 'mirage' of an individual and soon something of a mystery even to his two God-fearing neighbours. The label 'recluse' seemed to fit the new-comer in what was a quaint backwater – and there are several in rural Wales – where nothing much ever happened and, seemingly, never would.

Others, who enjoyed a quiet joke with friends in the local pubs – of which there were three – were not so compassionate and wondered why he hadn't chosen a concealed cave somewhere in the Outer Hebrides or a remote burial mound among the shifting sand-dunes in North Africa. And if shifting sand-dunes were not to his liking, why not a remote hut, better if inaccessible, high amid the Atlas Mountains in Morocco? Not one of the locals ever asked those who chose such locations 'why Morocco?' but to those who had never left mid-Wales, it supposedly sounded as distant and as remote as northern Tibet, the so-called 'roof of the world', where indeed, recluses, hermits and soul-seeking travellers do go and even despite the expulsion of the Dalai Lama are still made welcome.

It was well-known that most of the locals had little time for those they called 'eccentrics' or 'social misfits' and one or two were rather inventive as to other such places people like Noah should go: Alcatraz, Robyn Island, Vesuvius, Chernobyl, even the lost city of Atlantis! Ex-Solicitor and Former Mayor Hugh Dyfed Thomas, who had seen Noah just the once, was convinced that he had the 'look of a fugitive' and most likely had had dealings with international mafia agencies. Called 'Humpty-Dumpty' by his crony drinking pals, friendly but morbidly obese, Hugh Thomas loved the sound of his own voice and said that when he had some free time, he would 'google Interpol', sure that he would come up with something about their mysterious newcomer.

"To date, however" – he would sigh in his fluent Welsh tongue to his bar friends – "I haven't found a stitch, absolutely nothing, zilch, but I will. Just watch this space."

Speculation and rumour about Noah's 'former life' gave rise to a great deal of gossip and bawdy humour in the small-town pubs but also in neighbouring villages, too. Very soon and totally unaware of it, Noah had become a *'bête noire'* in cafes, restaurants and pubs, especially among the more mature population. With the young, however, Noah, although largely ignored, was seen as 'a harmless old fart'. The more learned among them who had studied al Latin called him 'Sir Flatulence' and left it at that. In their eyes, every town has its fair share of eccentrics and 'country-bumpkins' and Noah was one of such, but so what?

Although totally unaware of his undeserved notoriety, Noah deliberately kept himself to himself and spent his days in silent study; he very much enjoyed facing a blank page while holding a pencil and watching thoughts arise and fall in his 'talking head'. While others pored over crosswords, word-games, their mobiles, read the tabloids for horseracing and football results or, when looking for bargains and special offers, flicked through one of those glossy food-fashion magazines given away freely in supermarkets, he preferred to engage in what he termed 'creative viewing', his euphemism for silent meditation. And when he did put pen to paper, it was to write a poem, a short story or an aphorism, all of which he told himself were 'meditations' that he found therapeutic and which he firmly believed, especially as he got older, deserved to be read by a much wider audience. Whether he included in such an imaginary audience the likes of Hugh Dyfed Thomas and his drinking cronies, we will never know for sure, but they were all in for a deep shock. Keep reading to discover why.

From boyhood, Noah had kept a journal and when much later in life, he felt in a reflective mood, he would dip into his early journals (he had several) to re-connect with the things and events he had seen or done decades ago, most of which he had forgotten, but not all, because every life has events that live with one until the grave and beyond. In such readings, he was always reminded of the impermanence of things, nothing more so than of our feelings and our thoughts and the judgements we make based on those thoughts and feelings 'as they occur'. Ruminating on his early scribblings, he soon realized that it was our thoughts that dictated our lives and that they seemed to go round in never-ending circles inside our head. He also soon concluded that we were *their* unthinking slaves and so *he* sought ways and means to beat them at their own game and become the ruler of his kingdom of thoughts and, if he could achieve that, he would inevitably become the master of his actions. It sounded like a good plan and so he kept to it, religiously. He sought this remedy because while circling thoughts jostled for attention within him, he was simultaneously aware of a deep yearning for permanence, stability and inner peace.

In such periods that never lasted long of what he came to call 'wakeful awareness', he saw himself as an 'automaton' endowed with the power of movement and thus able to respond to the stimuli of his sense organs. And that was it. But that vision of himself inevitably led to feelings of growing dissatisfaction because something told him he was much more – or ought to be – than an automated machine. But what? and how could he really discover his true self, the real Noah, the maths teacher who had become a recluse in rural mid-Wales where allegedly there were more sheep than people? It was a question that never left him. It ran in his head like an unseen subterranean stream deep below street level and deeper than his level of wakeful consciousness; would he one day, perhaps, find an answer? And if he did, then what? For he was also aware that deeply sought answers to deeply felt questions can sometimes open a can of worms which proves ten times worse than having no answer! But Noah was old-school, a fighter, a man who preferred to be both self-sufficient and self-reliant. His journals or diaries show this and if we have time to read them all, we may find an answer of sorts to the question that never left him: would he ever discover his true self, the real identity of a nobody named Noah Azrael Salmon? But more to the point: why had he ever been born? Was there any purpose to our birth? Such questions led him on a quest that was to define his life, especially when in the 'autumn' of that life, as one of his journal entries puts it.

Noah had become a disciplined bookworm and loved reading biographies of people whom he believed had found their purpose in life; such people, so he believed, and only a few every generation, had done most for humanity. Such lives, so he thought, deserved his full-time study and deepest appreciation: but not only *his* time and appreciation but those of every thinking person on the planet. How else are we to leave this world a better place than when we entered it? His love of reading meant his deep respect for silence which, for him at least, was not only a prerequisite for study but was a much-needed virtue to be cultivated. He pitied students who, in order to study, mistakenly believe they need 'background music and their mobiles'. He claimed such souls lived in 'fear of silence' and those for whom such a claim was true, he advised immediate counselling and therapy. How can such souls, immersed in their texting or addicted to 'background wall-paper music', ever realize that only through silent study can anything worth reading or learning be achieved? Moreover – and this was inherent in his viewpoint – silent study also allows one to look inside the heart of what's being read – a novel? a textbook? a scientific paper? or even a children's fairy-tale or comic strip – and really helps with the comprehension of the material being read. And that is lost on those who have their mobiles on twenty-four-seven or whose concentration is 'weakened' by background music, baroque or not. But in his eyes, much more is 'lost' to us all because and here I am quoting Noah, *'the universe is constantly trying to tell us something, the knowing of which could, in that moment of awareness, change everything. And that change would mark that day as the "first day of the rest of his or her life".'*

After all, is it not true that there is no place that doesn't see us, all the time? Noah wanted such souls, lost in the forests of ever-changing thought, to look inside themselves, become introspective, even if only for three or four minutes and thus become aware of their experiences as they happened. If we all could do this, the meaning of those experiences would not be lost. It was a noble and magnanimous wish but often fell on deaf ears. And that's why he had a 'thing' about mobiles; they were a major reason people failed to look inside their own hearts and heads. "The world is full of gadgetry," he would occasionally say to his tolerant neighbours, "full of cars, radios, TVs, computers and now the mobile. Believe you me: mobiles are the opium of the people, especially of the young."

But not all was bad news: public reference libraries had banned all mobiles – radios were no longer a threat – and many schools had forbidden their use in the classroom and playground. "But how many of us nowadays," he would ask himself, "young and old alike, sleep-walk to our destination, whether school, work-place, pub, cinema or a friend's house, because of the mobile's multiple uses, especially chatting and texting?" And if neither of such modern 'curses' is the culprit then another opium, that of music, no matter which kind, rap, pop, dance, film or a hotchpotch mixture of the lot, does the same trick.

'Lost' in the technology of mobiles, most of us are all too often totally unaware of our neighbours – even if they, too, are sleepwalkers – or of our physical surroundings. We become mindless robots, a state of being that can – and so often does – lead to errors of judgement, painful accidents, road-rage and to countless, senseless arguments. For Noah, the mind was also a sense organ, but when the mind becomes the mobile's willing slave and not its master, troubles lie ahead. At this stage, the willing reader must be asking himself this simple question; with such thoughts and considerations as these, how can it be that septuagenarian Noah is seen as a 'villain of the peace'? An excellent question, for it points to the unbridled power of rumour, gossip, speculation and ignorance that thrive so gamely in the minds of the multitude. Was this the prime reason why 'recluse Noah' kept himself to himself?

In the evenings, he would listen to oriental chants as well as classical music and especially to well-known arias from his favourite operas. Those few who knew him also knew he was an out-and-out 'Mozart-man'; if pushed, he would willingly admit to enjoying the works of Verdi, Puccini, Bellini and Tchaikovsky. There were other composers, but those others he viewed as 'second division' players, a viewpoint his best of opera friends couldn't accept. But he didn't mind for he recognised that 'tastes in music differed as much as palates', and he was right.

His only neighbours who were also his closest friends ran the local Spiritualist Church and claimed that he also had 'a soft spot' for country western music, but this has never been corroborated. In fact, his only relative, a distant cousin who had emigrated to southern Spain in the 1990s and was still living there, disagreed, saying that Noah had always enjoyed 'church music', especially Gregorian chants and had 'abandoned' country western when he discovered opera and that was in his mid-thirties. We know this from Casey (the distant cousin mentioned above), who tells us that Noah discovered Mozart 'through a friend' who had given Noah two tickets to go to Covent Garden; the opera was the *Marriage of Figaro*. It was an epiphany, a real baptism of the spirit; unsurprisingly thereafter and for a period of three years, Noah went to every Mozart opera 'on show' in England. Whatever the production, school, local operatic society, a travelling troupe or a rehearsal, he would go and be 'in heaven' for three hours or so. His enthusiasm for Mozart and his music knew no bounds and he behaved like one of those born-again evangelical Christians who, in the 80s and 90s, transformed orthodox services by dancing in the aisles and by plucking their guitar strings in front of the sacred altar, and even in the pulpit!

His neighbours also knew that Noah made a point of going to Salzburg every summer to attend the Mozart season. Furthermore, Noah's passion for anything and everything 'Mozartian' had led him to study German and he spoke it very well, so well, indeed, that the locals in Salzburg thought he came from northern Germany. Among his possessions, he had... but we have to stop here for readers will now be 'up in arms' wondering who is this Casey character? And what has he to do with what we are reading about Noah? The answer is simple. Very shortly after his return from his last annual visit to Salzburg, Noah had a 'turn for the worse' and died peacefully in his sleep! He was found by his two Spiritualist neighbour friends who had keys to the cottage and visited him every Saturday morning without fail.

The two neighbours had been told about Casey – it seems Noah had no other relative alive or near – and so they contacted Casey and told him of Noah's 'passing on' as they always put it, and so he came to their small town near Brecon 'to sort things out'. He had managed to book a time-friendly air flight that included car-hire through a well-known cheap flight company from Alicante to Cardiff. On arrival, he picked up his Fiat 500 and drove safely to near the Brecon Beacons. He didn't know then that his stay would stretch to some five months.

The arrival of Casey marks the first major turning-point in what will become 'our remarkable meeting' with Noah, because it is what Casey discovers of his eccentric relative that becomes the reading matter, a novel, that Casey would soon deem worthy of publication.

In brief, from this point on in chapter one, we the readers will have to rely heavily on Casey to help us unlock the 'mysterious and very often misunderstood' life of his cousin Noah. And we can do that because they had been in 'contact' loosely over the last five years via infrequent e-mails and the odd telephone conversation, mainly on birthdays and at Xmas time. Their contact was minimal to say the least, but we have precious little other contacts to turn to if we wish to further our understanding of a highly unusual human being. When Noah died – and his death was both sudden and unexpected – it was left to Casey to sift through his cousin's belongings, sort out his will and assets and finally to sell his quaint cottage-style home, one of two, in a *cul-de-sac* on the edge of town. And it was during this sad but busy period when Casey and the locals were to discover things about Noah that caught everyone by surprise, especially his closest neighbours.

CHAPTER 2

For a start, Casey quickly found a bundle of diaries neatly stacked inside a drawer of Noah's study desk. On top were his PC, a printer and a land-line telephone; a well-thumbed *Oxford English Reference Dictionary* held pride of place at one end of the desk that was both spacious and spotlessly clean. It seems that Noah belonged to that growing army of 'dust-freaks'; his aversion to it made him dust-clean every room in his home every single day, in particular his study and bedroom. This significant fact was told to Casey by Noah's Spiritualist neighbours who from their weekly visits knew his habits and most of what they courteously called his 'idiosyncrasies'. When Noah was once gently questioned by his affable neighbour Evangeline about the 'dust-thing', his reply to her was that "dust carries germs and germs kill; because of dust, mortality surrounds us all the time, twenty-four-seven!"

What he didn't tell his sympathetic neighbour was that both his maternal and paternal grandparents had died from cholera. Noah had felt particularly close to both sets of grandparents and, when very young, would love to listen to them talk about life as they knew it when they were growing up. Even though all this had passed 'aeons' ago, he retained very vivid memories of their homes, their speech-patterns, their dress-code and their hobbies which had been gardening, bee-keeping, sewing, choir-singing and star-gazing. Their aim had always been to be 'as self-sufficient as possible' and so gardening for them meant growing vegetables and having fruit trees rather than cultivating aromatic plants and flowers or tending to an impeccably trim lawn. Both grandmothers baked their own bread, knitted their own clothes and were competent at sewing repairs. And every Sunday went to church services morning and evening and were the backbone of the church-choir. But they were now long-dead and Noah had never ever made one visit to their family graves.

"You can't change the past," was what he used to say, "and so it's best left alone. The only thing of importance to us human beings now is the here-and-now. Look after that and the future will take care of itself."

From such comments, it was clear that all that really mattered to him (and in his view, to everybody around him on Planet Earth) was the 'present moment', the time of now: 'now-ness' as he liked to call it, because 'only now is real'. His neighbours soon realised that Noah tried to live his life in accord with this belief which they saw as one of his guiding principles. And they said as much to Casey who soon became a regular visitor to their spic-and-span domicile during his stay at Noah's quaint cottage home.

It should be said that mortality, as a topic, really appealed to Evangeline; after all, she had visited several homes to liberate 'trapped souls' who needed to 'cross over', as she put it. For her, ghosts were a reality, but her prime concern was to release 'souls in pain', souls that for some reason had been unable to 'pass on'; such souls she claimed – but only if you pressed her – were often of those who had died in tragic circumstances; a road accident, a house fire, a brutal murder, an earthquake and similar, and of such cases there were too many to report. So, her contact with the 'living dead' as she described such beings was on-going, but she far preferred to emphasise the 'living spirit within each of us' rather than the death of the physical body. "We are all ghosts in a machine," she was keen to tell anyone she met, "and the machine is our physical body and everyone knows all machines have a built-in obsolescence."

That said, had she asked Noah – but for some reason never did – why he tended to focus on finality, she would have heard him say, "It's only by focussing on one's end can one truly appreciate the life we have and lead." And no doubt she would have agreed with him, for that made good sense to her and also to her husband, Craig.

Although Noah may have pinpointed his gaze on mortality and on the inevitable transience of things, the Noah she knew and grew to admire was not afraid of dying: not at all. She knew that one of his favourite literary quotes ran thus: '*Cowards die many times before their death.*' Neither Evangeline nor Casey knew where it came from; both had read far less than Noah and so it was to be expected that he would occasionally say something that neither had heard or read before. And that fact, *inter alia*, both for Evangeline and her loving husband, was what drew them to him. Noah was a veritable walking encyclopaedia of refrains and quotes, dates and names, especially culled from Latin authors and found scattered, as was soon to be realized, throughout his diaries. He seemed to have had a prodigious memory and whenever he quoted something, it was word perfect and he always seemed to know its source. Did he have that rare gift of a photographic memory? Let us keep this question in mind, or on the back-burner as the current expression goes, as we progress through what Casey comes to uncover in his cousin's hitherto unknown and unread personal memoirs.

Without doubt, it is Noah's memoirs written in diary-form that immediately grip Casey; although he had gone to sort out

Noah's will, his papers, clothes, items of value as well as 'sundries' and sell the cottage – its proceeds were to go to a school for the blind in a near-by village – he had no idea that Noah had kept a diary from his school-days that ran into at least ten thick note-pads of A4 paper. Indeed, the last entry was May 18, three days before his 'passing' in his own home. His neighbours had made their weekly Saturday morning visit (being much older, he had given them a key to his home in case of any emergency) and found him 'asleep', that is what they thought at first, in his four-poster bed. But no, he had *'died while quietly reading a book on cosmology'* that lay on his bedside table. The neighbours immediately called the paramedics who arrived in under twelve minutes and took him by ambulance to the nearest hospital. The police were also informed and, although they took statements, they waited for an official medical report. Within a week, the obligatory post-mortem declared that Noah had died from 'natural causes', not uncommon in the Far East but unusual in so-called advanced western societies. His neighbours and friends were happy that he had met such a gentle 'exit' from this lower world of shadows, dreams and germs. Although no one dared to mention it at the wake, they all recognised that 'Uncle Noah' (his physical body was what they all meant) would quickly dissolve into the very dust he had loathed since childhood. Dust eventually had won, but that fact did not weigh on Noah's mind when he was burnt to ashes and that simple truth made them all smile in his honour.

    They all knew that he'd always eaten a healthy diet (at university in St Andrews, he had become a strict vegetarian), exercised daily, was not by any means obese and meditated every morning. When told of these things later, Casey, a staunch believer in a Supreme Intelligence or Spirit that overlooked all life everywhere and not only on Planet Earth, told himself that 'the ways of the Lord are indeed unfathomable'. In his hand, he was holding Noah's freshly minted death certificate that claimed that 'natural causes' were the cause of death; it was duly signed, dated and stamped for all to see. Casey made three photo-copies of the certificate; as executor of Noah's will and assets, it was a wise decision.

In subsequent conversations with Noah's genteel neighbours, Casey could see that both were greatly saddened at their enigmatic neighbour's 'moving or passing on' as they always described the event of death, yet were convinced he had gone to a better place and therefore also felt an inner joy, a joy that they were accustomed not to show.

"And why is that?" he asked them.

Their reply surprised him; they said they knew that death, bereavement, burial or cremation are all associated with sadness in western societies, but because of their spiritual beliefs, they both felt serenity and gladness; any soul that is freed from decay and death, which is the lot of every human being, deserves to be celebrated.

He agreed and believes that their viewpoint really demands more respect and consideration than is often the case. Evangeline's long-time partner, Craig from Dumfries, was a good-hearted, well-intentioned individual, an architect by profession who had come to the enlightened conclusion that life is all about transience, suffering, decay and death. He had spent several years in Sri Lanka in his youth and shared that nation's belief in the Four Noble Truths and the Eightfold Path. In fact, he had tried to live his life following the Buddha's guidelines or teachings. His deep belief in their everyday practicality was shared by his down-to-earth wife, the only daughter of a

Salvation Army major named Wayne. It was the major who proudly wore his crest upon a red epaulet badge until his dying day. It should be mentioned that Craig totally believed in rebirth and because of this belief, he secretly yearned to end the relentless wheel of life and death *'this time round'*, as he put it, and finally 'merge' with his Creator and live in eternal peace and bliss. Apparently, he had been born with a burning desire to be subsumed by the 'unknown and unseen Creator' of the universe – indeed, of all universes – the Supreme Energy or Being, in which all actions allegedly originate and to which, so he believed, all actions return. When in Sri Lanka and later in China, he had met several devout Buddhists and so, on his return to the UK, he turned to Buddhism. When he met his wife-to-be, he joined her group of friends and soon became a co-worker. But he had no desire to abandon his allegiance to Buddhism and so he continued with his acceptance, and simple practice, of the basic precepts given as guidelines for everyday living by Buddha. He especially valued the daily practice of meditation and in time persuaded his wife to join him. She undertook courses and over the years became totally convinced of its use in her life and in her work. And because Craig saw no real conflict with the established beliefs of Spiritualism, he soon became an active member of the Spiritualist community. When asked about his personal beliefs, Craig always claimed that he found the blend deeply satisfying and much more 'spiritual than a bottle of rum, brandy or a good noggin of distilled whisky'.

He shared with his wife a love of brass bands and both played the trombone and euphonium very well. But for some reason he had never told Evangeline, a former captain with the Sally Army and still very proud of her 'two-stars-upon-a-red-epaulet badge', of his yearning to be subsumed by the Creator of the visible and invisible worlds within and beyond our galaxy; he wanted his present life to be his 'final embodiment' because he had read somewhere that those who make the Supreme Spirit their 'only refuge and devoutly seek release from decay and death' will attain their soul's release and enjoy eternal bliss with the Creator of all worlds, the living force that animates all things everywhere.

Casey was to engage in long conversations with Noah's nearest neighbours and accepted their invitation to visit their church and meet its deeply devout members. As mentioned, Casey was to stay five months in Noah's house until it was finally sold and so, every Sunday – and sometimes on weekdays, too – he accompanied his neighbours to their church and, quite quickly, as was his wont, was able to build up a substantial 'picture' of cousin Noah. But the real flesh and bones of that picture were to emerge from the 'secret diaries' that Casey began to read and soon wanted everybody else to read, too. The more he read, the more convinced he became that the diaries deserved an audience that went beyond Noah's quiet cul-de-sac and quaint neighbourhood where he spent the 'autumn of his life'. In short, Casey was soon to share Noah's thoughts about his 'meditations' and became convinced that the diaries ought to be published, and once published, translated into every civilised tongue on the planet! And that ambitious objective deepened as he read through each and every journal. It was something of a surprise to him that such an objective would ever enter his head; it proved to be one of several surprises yet to be unlocked and we, as readers, will have to exercise patience before they are revealed…

In brief, the rest of this account concerns the reading of the diaries written by Noah Azrael Salmon, who on the outside comes across as a self-effacing maths teacher who spent his retirement years in 'silent reflective study'. And part of that 'reflective study' entailed the updating of his diaries; it also entailed serious reading, attempts at creative writing and in listening to the radio. He enjoyed such programmes as a 'book at bedtime', open debates and to programmes of classical music.

"But hold on a minute," says the impatient reader, "let's start at the beginning. We've read what his neighbours have said of him and that's useful. We've also just read that the picture that comes across of Noah as self-effacing stands in sharp conflict with the cruel comments and remarks made by some of the locals in the small town's bars and pubs. And it may be that Casey's readings will reveal to us, the readers, a much more authentic picture and personality of the man behind the journals. But we want to make up our own minds. So, please, let's now go directly to the journals themselves and we do mean, now, please!"

And that is what will now be done. So let's turn now to the lived life of Noah Salmon, a life that from the very outset both entertains and challenges cousin Casey; in fact, the reading of the diaries was to change Casey Roebuck forever.

As he reads them, he enters into a sort of 'dialogue' with the author, resulting in a text that from the very outset has a dual perspective; add to that the perspective of the unseen narrator, the perspective of other characters (Noah's friends, colleagues, neighbours) as well as the crucial perspective of each individual reader and the result is a work of multiple voices and voices mean viewpoints. If Casey was to be changed forever by his reading of the journals, cannot the same be said of every reader, too?

CHAPTER 3

What first caught Casey's eye as he began Book One of the diaries was a statement that had been pinned to the inside cover; dated 7 July 1984, the very year Noah reached forty and 7 July was his date of birth. The statement, not typed but written in beautiful calligraphic script, read as follows:

A question hangs over every life. Invariably, it's the same question for everybody although experience formulates it differently for each of us. It has three aspects: who am I? what is the world? and what is my relationship to it? Consciously or not, every person born on Planet Earth (and why not on other planets in our solar system, too?) has to face it. And that's because the question is inherent in the human psyche. We are born with it, just as we are born with hands and feet, arms and legs. Some may choose to ignore the question, others may prefer to deny it, or even laugh at it, but it won't go away because it can't; it's tied to our DNA.

No name or source had been given but due to its place of prominence, the statement clearly meant a great deal to Noah: it was also very possible that the statement was of his own making. Curiosity then made Casey sift quickly through each of the diaries and he saw that the same statement was attached to all of his journals, except the last, that was also by far the shortest, and had as its final entry the date of 15 May, three days before his unexpected 'passing on'. He then slowly re-read the eye-catching statement, not once but twice, and rightly concluded that it was meant to serve as a 'mini-prologue'. He found that its contents appealed to his innate sense of curiosity – he always enjoyed reading things that were 'thought-provoking or strangely different' – and he put that down to his early reading of comics where all sorts of weirdly unexpected events occur, as much as to his natural thirst for knowledge.

Ever since primary school, he had enjoyed learning what he was taught, whether arithmetic, reading, geography, religious education and so on and he was good at it. In class tests, he was always in the first three and that pleased his teachers, his parents but most of all himself. Luckily, he had a good memory and that helped him in everything. We could say he was a model pupil – but he wouldn't say that about himself – and was well-liked by both fellow pupils and the teaching staff. That said, above all else, he yearned to travel and meet people from all over and to be able to communicate with them. And that yearning sparked his interest and talent in foreign languages: he began with Latin followed by Spanish, French, German and Italian and then, much later in life, wanting to be 'different', studied Hindi and Mandarin.

Underlying all his language studies and language courses in foreign lands lay an interest in the very questions to which his cousin Noah had given special emphasis in his diaries. And he agreed with Noah; the question is born with us and does indeed consist of three distinct aspects, each of which needs to be addressed. He viewed the question as the cross that every thinking person – among whom he modestly included himself – has to bear. For, undoubtedly, Casey was a 'thinking person'; so much so that if any reader were to visit his home, he would find shelf after shelf of works written by philosophers, especially the Greeks, and nineteenth-century German thinkers, in particular Kant, Schopenhauer, Nietzsche and the Austrian writer Ludwig Wittgenstein. Due to such an interest, Casey knew he had met a soul-mate in distant cousin Noah and that he, Casey Roebuck, was the ideal person to read and make sense of Noah's interests and personal memoirs that filled the notepads. Besides, there was no other relative able and willing to carry out the sale of the country-style cottage, settle the estate, sort out the assets, sift through personal belongings and lastly, go through diaries which he very quickly began to see as a delayed attempt at an 'autobiography'.

And so, when not at the solicitor's, or with the Spiritualists, or with trustees of the centre for the blind (an unconfirmed source claimed that Noah wanted to leave any monies from the sales of his assets to the nearest centre for the blind) or with estate agents, or even watching late-night telly, Casey would turn off his mobile and would carefully read for two or three hours, (sometimes even longer) and would invariably make notes. His note-taking enabled him to remember the diverse contents of his diary-readings more clearly; in the same way that the statement appended to the inside of the opening of Book One needs careful reading and consideration – after all, Noah was not writing for the tabloids where photos very often mean more than the 'stories' they illustrate. Casey soon discovered that ex-maths teacher, Noah, wrote material that was original, soul-stirring, instructive and at times highly amusing. He also took delight in Noah's turn of phrase, clarity of thought and expression that he used to describe the very things and events Casey liked to read about.

The first thing of interest about Diary One was its date; September 1955, London. And added to the inside page beneath the 'prologue-statement' was a photo of Noah when c.eleven years old, wearing a school uniform, with tie and blazer. Slim, round faced with very wavy hair, and with a smile to die for, Noah seemed to be a happy-go-lucky pupil at a comprehensive school in West London. We know he enjoyed school-life and discipline and showed a talent for mathematics, technical drawing (that he considered 'pure art') and sports: at least that is what his final primary school report claimed that had been tucked inside an unsealed envelope. But attached to the report was a brief letter to Noah's parents written by Noah's form teacher, a Mr William Crookes. In the letter, Mr Crookes makes some highly unusual observations, as curious as they are unexpected, which now follow verbatim:

"Noah needs careful watching. In his thoughts, amusements and hobbies he is not like any other boy in his class. Although he can do the things the other boys of his age usually do – and do well – I believe Noah can do many things that the rest can't do. And because his real interest is in these 'other things', I note that, of late, he has tended to isolate himself from his class-mates. It seems to me he has, sadly, found no-one to share his enthusiasms for things that normally appeal to much older boys, even undergraduates; his interest in mathematical problems, in invention and in 'other-worldly' things, set him aside. I believe that one day, people will take note of his achievements. I also believe that Noah is aware of his unusual interests and talents."

But then a gap occurs in the diary followed by a hair-raising entry; *Mum left dad and hasn't been seen for six weeks; father says I'm to be sent to a boarding-school in Kent next week.* The entry was dated 12 February 1956.

And indeed the next entry, dated 27 February, gives details about the school: St Joseph's Boarding School, Orpington, Kent. It also served as a day-school for local Roman Catholic pupils. Noah readily accepted that his life had changed and that he had to adapt to new environs in a school with different teachers who follow a different core curriculum. That said, he seems to have had enjoyed his stay in Kent and did so because he was 'good at both sports and academic subjects', especially at maths and physics and represented the school at football, cricket and at athletics; apparently he was a good sprinter. But not all was a 'bed of lotus flowers' as he later was to describe this episode in his school-life: when thirteen, he was struck down by chickenpox and spent 'two awful months in Orpington General Hospital'. He really believed he was going to die – and so did his doctors, initially – but his 'time had not come' and he eventually made a full recovery. No one knew why his recovery took so long and that was worrying, not only to the medical staff but also to his teachers because they knew that no 'intelligent pupil' wants to fall behind his peers and class-mates in schoolwork.

But both his schoolteachers and the parents of others in his class and dormitory had the shock of their lives when one junior medic spoke out of turn, claiming that Noah was not suffering from chickenpox, but from cholera! Despite a world of difference in both diseases, everybody, especially the school authorities and senior medics, went through a period of deep anxiety. When, to the relief of all involved, Noah finally recovered, he returned to his classes and 'caught up with his school-work in no time at all'. It was an achievement that seemed to confirm Mr Crookes' comments made in his brief letter to Noah's parents some two years before. Reading this, the question that crossed Casey's mind was this: what other things would Noah do to further confirm his primary school form-teacher's observations?

But the illness left Noah with an absolute horror of hospitals, infirmaries, clinics and anything to do with medicines, pills, tablets and vaccinations. He even baulked at taking the ever-popular 'Fisherman's friend' lozenge-sweet that, ever since his student days, everyone took at the slightest cough, hiccup, sneeze or sniffle. But not Noah: although he enjoyed the 'fresh mint taste' of the lozenge, he stubbornly refused to accept it was a 'quick-fix' cure. No, he far preferred to focus on preventative measures and so, in early autumn, a morning cup of herbal tea that included lemon, ginseng and pure honey would be found on his kitchen table. Without doubt, however, the most damaging consequence of his illness was that thereafter, and to his dying day, he lived in fear of germs. He knew they were everywhere and had often heard the doctors and nurses say as much. And whenever they spoke of germs, they looked, so he observed, as if they were speaking of the guillotine or the pains of hell! Really! And so if the word 'germs' filled the medical staff with such dread and horror, what was he to infer? He quickly discovered that germs were part of life's seamless fabric on Planet Earth and, like the presence of the Almighty, albeit invisible, were everywhere! It was a horrible discovery to be made by one so young and so talented and because of both factors, so vulnerable.

To his credit, it seems that, after his stint in hospital, Noah somehow was able to keep his phobia to himself. When, later in adolescence, he heard the term 'germ-warfare', he did not see it as others did, as a military threat or as a possible deterrent but willy-nilly accepted it as part of our daily struggle; an unpleasant but unavoidable fact of life. Of this he was convinced and explains, in later life, his passion – many would say obsession – with house-cleaning. He was to spend a mini-fortune on a wide variety of disinfectants, bleaches, house-cleaning products, airsprays and rubber gloves. And he was happy to do so because he had single-handedly (so it seemed to him) declared war on humanity's worst enemy: *dust*. Every speck had to be removed, whatever the surface, metal, plastic, fabric, wood, tile or ceramic and removed as swiftly as humanly possible. And so that is what Noah did on a daily basis, but no matter how well he cleaned and removed spot after spot, it didn't stop him the following day repeating the exercise even more thoroughly, if that were at all possible! No home, flat or office in the kingdom was more thoroughly cleaned. And that meant hard work and so, in later life when his energies were not so abundant, aware that he needed help, divine or otherwise, he even scoured the ancient calendars and almanacs to see if there was a 'saint of dusting', but he never found one!

There was not one place in his home, garage or loft where dust could accumulate; every nook and cranny was scrubbed daily so that not even one spider had been seen for years. And yet, in his equally prim and proper garden, he loved watching how spiders, in total silence and with amazing skill and speed, wove their intricate webs and would then keep out of sight until a victim, a fly, wasp or ladybird, for example, flew innocently into the web and became the next meal! As a youngster, he was often seen catching a lady bird, or a fly, spinning 'in helicopter mode' (because it was dying) and would then throw the insect into the middle of the web just to see the spider appear from nowhere. And then the fun began; he was spellbound watching the spider 'mummify' the helpless object that, when wrapped tightly in its woven strait-jacket, guaranteed a future feast for the wily predator.

Yes, dust was his pet hate. Indeed, every book he ever bought had to have a dust-jacket which he wiped clean as part of his 'house-work'. Furthermore – and this is no exaggeration – he took no delight in any bird or animal having a dust-bath. Had we been able to look inside Noah's head, we would have seen how, in his subconscious, he indissolubly linked dust with ashes. When very young and at school, a rather pious schoolteacher had taught him that we all 'turn to ashes' and it was something he'd never forgotten. He had read of missionaries in Sri Lanka and in rural China who had heard of villagers meeting their deaths in dust-storms which they called 'dust-devils'. Whether entities called devils were really made of dust was less important than the fact that many had been killed by them! In brief, it was blatantly obvious to Casey that Noah and dust did not see eye to eye; no accord between them was ever possible. So much so that among his unique collection of 'oddities' was a medieval text about the history of face-masks as found in Europe and in Asia. Underneath this text stood a WW2 gas-mark that sat flanked on both sides by a shrunken human head; both heads came from a tribe living in Bolivia and had been bought from an antiques dealer now living in Amsterdam. The two shrunken heads were a special favourite of his Spiritualist neighbours. If there is time, Casey will tell us more about Noah's 'strange collection' of what most would call 'oddities', but only if such a mention enhances the text that is fast evolving into a highly unusual novel.

Apart from his one serious illness of chickenpox (no way was it cholera), the remainder of Noah's life at the boarding school seems to have sailed smoothly by. And so, when only fifteen (church-run boarding schools turfed out its inmates at fifteen), he left with nothing except his annual school reports (three in all) and a healthy willingness to be of use to society. He had the energy and motivation to work for his living and make a contribution to the world he lived in, sentiments not commonly found among fifteen-year olds nowadays. With the help of his father, he soon found work in a food factory in London; it was where his father was also employed. No surprise then that Noah, after leaving secondary school, stayed with his father. After all, where else could he go? A chapter of his early life had ended; school had given way to the world of work, a brutal transition for any fifteen-year old. And so, just like his father, indeed no different to the vast majority of mankind, he was now a wage-slave, like it or not...

CHAPTER 4

English law decreed that all young people, who were employed and under eighteen, had to attend day college once a week. In time, he enjoyed college work and life much more than a dead-end job that paid a pittance. And so, 'moved by the spirit', so it seems and with reference to nobody but to himself, he one day arranged a meeting with Miss Darby, head of the department, and bravely asked for a pay-rise.

"A pay-rise, boy, but that's out of the question!"

When told that the position was fixed and that no rise in pay was permissible, he took the momentous decision to leave work and return to full-time study; in so doing and after a very studious eighteen months, he obtained eight O Levels and thus was eligible to do A Levels and found a college in Holborn that offered one-year intensive A Level courses. He was in a hurry, having lost ground in a brain-dead job and pinned all his hopes on a one-year, instead of the customary two-year, A-Level course. It was a godsend of an opportunity and he seized it with both hands. He chose to study maths, physics and Latin and passed all three important subjects in the one year; it was a stupendous achievement, highly unusual, a fact that deeply impressed the interviewing panel at St Andrews. He had worked, so he claimed during his interview, *'harder than any Trojan or any Greek island donkey'* and it was true, but the real reason why he had done so was because he found life at home with his father intolerable, mentally and socially! He simply had to escape and so worked his socks off to obtain the grades necessary to gain admission at either St Andrews or at Durham (his favoured two of the five listed on his application form). He had chosen traditional universities as far from London as possible. When St Andrews offered him a place he was inwardly ecstatic but kept his feelings to himself; he had no wish to upset his father who had had no education beyond secondary level and was far more interested in beer, cigarettes, greyhound- and horse-racing than in the enigmas and challenges of maths and physics or in the declensions of irregular nouns in classical Latin. But Noah was careful not to criticise: neither parent had ever had the educational opportunities available in the 1960s to so-called 'war-babies'. Was such an understanding of, and compassion for, his parents' predicament an early sign of his latent readiness for life's guidelines as given by Lord Buddha? Read on and find out. You won't regret it!

And so it was that Noah spent three very happy years at St Andrews. He didn't mind the colder 'weather north of the border', that brought snow, icy winds, shorter evenings in winter, heavy rainfall and incessant grey sky-cover. He knuckled down to his studies, soon became known as a 'bookworm', enjoyed the sports on offer and made full use of the various university facilities, especially the well-stocked libraries. Such buildings offered him warmth, good lighting and access to texts that he would never be able to afford and so that is where he spent most of his day and evenings, leaving only to attend his lectures. That much is to be gleaned from his Book Two, but that said, entries in his diary covering these years are relatively scant; he spent his summer vacations working in factories (a toy factory and a paper-mill), on farms and in country pubs. But whatever the work, he made sure that he did some study every single day. Mention is made of student friends (but of no girl-friends) and of one teacher of maths who truly inspired him. Although he made good use of his time and clearly enjoyed his stay at university, he says almost nothing about Edinburgh, its festivals, traditions, New Year's 'fiestas' or about any of the great writers, scientists or medics who lived or had studied there. And Casey believed the reason for that is to be found in Noah's singlemindedness; he had little time for 'distractions' for that is how he saw discos, student parties, binge-drinking episodes and common student pranks. He hailed from a dysfunctional family, his background had been 'erratic' and his life to date had been a real struggle; he always 'felt he was fighting against the odds', as he saw it, and it was that firm conviction that made him focus totally on graduation. His unspoken fear of failure was almost as deep-seated as his fear of dust!

His future depended on his degree; without it, his life-choices would be cruelly limited – that's how he saw it. He had no desire to end up in another dead-end job, or become a slave to any factory owner. His not-so-distant experiences working in a paper-mill, toy and food factories had taught him what he *didn't* want from life. For him, life without prospects or options was no life, but slavery; qualifications, so he believed, would release him from the iron chains of servitude. And if he ever met Miss Right and wanted a family life, he would need to be able to support both in relative comfort. Scraping a wage, living from hand-to-mouth and wondering where the next meal was coming from did not figure on his agenda, but it was a daily reality for countless others. He was aware that such fears were never far from the surface; in fact, they pushed him to work even harder. The consequence was inevitable: in his fertile, undergraduate mind, nothing but nothing would take precedence over course-work.

And because intentions make one's world, his university life, both enjoyable and deservedly successful, it passed by without any traumas. He was also aware that most of the undergraduates at St Andrews had had a 'normal' upbringing; they came from stable families underpinned by love and affection and had spent two years doing their A Levels. And he was happy for them: that said, his heart was set on a first class honours degree, come what may, and that was to be followed by a post graduate certificate in education. He wanted to teach maths, especially to underprivileged pupils who had a flair for the subject but faced handicaps at home, and that is what he eventually did.

Little did he realise at the time of his university studies that underprivileged pupils often come from environments that militate against their aptitudes or aspirations. But let not Casey jump the gun. Let's keep with him as he reads the diaries and attempts to come to terms with their 'challenging' and unusual content. His reactions, comments and observations serve a very noble narrative purpose which is to add to, if not enrich, the journals' interest and appeal.

After his degree, Noah went on to get his teaching qualification at Sheffield university and found his first teaching post in Leeds, in a comprehensive school in one of the poorest districts in the city. One year later, his dream of assisting the underprivileged was in pieces, broken for ever. Every day had been a real struggle: the majority of pupils from sink-estates had an in-built aversion to the word 'math', never mind the nitty-gritty of the tests, assignments and the inherent difficulties of the subject. His pupils were content with knowing how to add, subtract and multiply; with these skills they were 'made for life' and they were, given the life they saw ahead of them. Their mind-set was more solid than Mount Everest and nothing could change it and so Noah, in time, gave up trying. If they knew how to count, how to work out the cost (rather than the value) of the things they wanted to buy (the latest pair of Levi's, sports shoes, T-shirt, leisure jacket or nail varnish), they were more than satisfied, but it also meant they showed no interest whatsoever in anything bordering on 'mathematical problem-solving exercises', algebra, trigonometry or geometry. Such questions that began *'If it takes four men to dig a trench in three days, how long...?'* were met with scorn and ridicule.

Some would shout out to him, *'Sir, why should anyone dig a hole when we have machines to do the work for us? Besides, what a boring job!'* And, of course, the whole class would then clap and stamp their feet and sing out in unison, saying, *'Yes, boring, boring, just like this class, boring, boring!'*

And when one day (and all this is recorded in his diary, Book Two) he was told by the most disruptive female student he'd ever met 'to get a proper job' and that her dad *'working in a local fruit market earned three times more than he did'*, he knew he had to get out. And so he resigned and did so before finding another post. Maths teacher Noah knew he was no front-line soldier. He had read of the awful plight of German soldiers fighting on the Eastern front against the Soviets in WW2 and sympathised greatly, but he had no wish to follow suit. And the image of the terrible conditions on the eastern front that he used to describe his experiences as a maths teacher in a comprehensive in Leeds is highlighted in the diary. This entry was followed by a chilling comment written in blood-red fountain pen ink that said:

Child-minding is what happens every day in our Secondary schools. Teaching, if it occurs but it doesn't, remains an illusion. Too many Chief Education Officers live in cuckoo-land!

It was clear to Casey that Noah, after only one year as a would-be dedicated teacher of maths, had come to breaking-point. His physical and mental health were on the line and there was no way that he would sacrifice both in a battle that couldn't be won. The odds against him, a solitary voice in a sea of hostile, resentful, prejudiced voices, were insurmountable. He had neither the strength of Hercules nor the bravado of Perseus, the rider of the winged wonder horse Pegasus, at his disposal. What peeved him most now was the realisation that in the course leading to his teaching qualification, nothing had ever been said about the uncouth attitudes and jungle classroom behaviour that he met on a daily basis! Not even during his three teaching practices had he ever met such resistance to the study of a core-subject that he loved with a passion. With hindsight, he acknowledged that those practices took place in the 'best schools' locally where parents made sure their offspring were well-behaved and so never impeded the teaching process; as a result, such 'motivated' pupils were well taught and deservedly obtained very good grades. But even these paled in comparison to grades obtained by fee-paying pupils sent to so-called 'public-schools'. As in everything else, money ruled the educational system, a system his colleagues called 'Bismarck's Battleship'. He had to run to the Oxford English Reference Dictionary to see who Bismarck was and what he'd done!

After one year in education, he knew that if he had children and he could afford the costs, his offspring would be sent to private schools. Such discoveries forced his hand: he knew he had to get out simply because current barbaric attitudes in *his* lessons (and he knew from other teachers that they also suffered) were beginning to undermine his love of maths and that is something he would never accept, come what may.

When he scoured the TES (*Times Educational Supplement*) looking for a suitable job, he discovered that the better paid jobs went to those with higher qualifications and so he began studying for a masters, part-time, at Manchester University. Fortunately, he had already found a job as assistant head of department of maths at a private boarding school near Chester and spent two 'sane and contented years' (his words from the same diary, Book Two) that enabled him to obtain his masters, and do so unstressed. Indeed, he found life as a teacher in a boarding-school much more relaxed, even 'normal'; his earlier experience as a boarder proved a huge advantage and he 'fitted in' nicely with the teaching staff; his pupils were multi-national, highly motivated, well-behaved and appreciated the efforts teachers made to help them secure the best grades possible. In such a 'civilised environment' (again, his words), Noah was able to study hard and accomplish his assignments in good time. His thesis was centred on the mature work of Tesla and so it was no surprise to Casey that works on and by Tesla were found in Noah's personal library. Apart from these and other snippets, little else is to be found in Book Two that 'explains' Noah, his personality, attitudes, viewpoints or lifestyle when in Cheshire. Book Three begins with his deserved appointment as Assistant Head of Department of Maths in a popular sixth form college very close to the town of Chorley near Preston.

Another chapter was about to begin in Noah's life that so far had been both eventful and unpredictable. No explanation is needed – indeed, none is given – as to why Noah, after the nightmare of Leeds and the heaven of Cheshire, chose a sixth form college over any return to a teaching job in secondary education; a return to front-line teaching was never an option.

But in a college, students had already chosen their A-Level subjects; so they were, supposedly, mature, committed and competent. What adventures or traumas would Noah meet as a new number two in a busy department in a bustling sixth form college in NE England was the question that immediately entered Casey's head. It seemed to Noah's curious reader-cousin that the diaries numbered from three onwards would count as the important ones in the gradual build-up of a life that was on the brink of 'opening up'.

CHAPTER 5

From his earliest days, Noah, so Casey found at the start of Book Three, had always enjoyed 'being outside' and exploring his immediate environment and beyond. It was something he had been born with, an integral part of his unique DNA and would admit as much – but only if asked – to his work-colleagues and later on, to his friends and neighbours. The circumambient universe meant much more to him than the locality he was born into or where he worked, played and had his being. Cheshire had been more environmentally agreeable than West London, Orpington and Leeds put together, but better than Cheshire was red-rose Lancashire in North-West England. He had always shown a keen interest in keeping fit and healthy, although he well knew that many fit people were not healthy and many healthy people were not fit. And so, when still a young teacher in Chorley, he joined a yoga class and went to classes twice a week. It was upon his yoga teacher's gentle suggestion to 'give vegetarianism a twirl' that after a two-month trial period, he became an out-and-out vegetarian, a fact that he highlights in bold red ink midway in Book Three of his diaries.

It was highlighted because he believed he had been re-baptised: he was now eating *manna* from heaven and drinking from Eden's sacred river – or was it a fountain? – the elixir of life. He claimed that Eden must have had a sacred river because all myths about Heaven tend to include one! Not only did he turn to a vegetarian diet, but he also joined a Rambler's Club and went hill-walking regularly. He found he was the youngest member by far and so he was pampered, but he had always preferred the company of those older than himself. And so with a vegetarian diet, rambling and weekly yoga classes, he warmed to life in Lancashire and thrived. In time, yoga became for him the physical exercise par excellence, better even than tantric sex and so he decided to become a yoga teacher, a course that took him four years to complete, part-time. While studying for his BWY (British Wheel of Yoga) qualification, a fellow-student alerted him to an intensive yoga course in Crete and so he went. It was another epiphany on his journey through this world that, as a pupil at primary school, he had been taught to view as a 'vale of tears'; a concept he didn't like, but it would never leave him. So, whether true or not, he lived with it but had found in yoga a practical cure for many of this world's ills.

And on his course in Crete, he met like-minded people and quickly made many new friends, many from the USA, Brazil and Australia, some of whom went every summer to Crete. And so, almost inevitably, Noah made a point of returning to Crete whenever possible. During one such summer course, he was destined to meet whom he describes as 'Miss Wonderful'; a graduate lawyer-linguist from Bristol university, fluent in Hindi and Urdu – her mother came from New Delhi and insisted on teaching Sunita, her only child, Hindi at home. Later on, Sunita went to a temple in Bristol and continued lessons in Hindi and Sanskrit, the language of Hinduism's most sacred texts. Her father, named Mark, was a lawyer from London but had moved to Bristol 'to be closer to Anjali'; the girl he loved and later married.

By all accounts, Sunita had had the ideal upbringing; she loved her parents but seemed to love school-work almost as much. Unsurprisingly, she excelled, and later at university, was top of her year. But the biggest feather in her cap – and this was something she occasionally voiced among other female friends and relatives – was the fact she had remained a virgin throughout. She quickly told Noah when they became 'good friends' that her virginity was to be her *'best and most precious present to her future husband'*. And so if Noah had any ideas of intimacy, it wouldn't happen without a wedding ring! She had her principles and stuck to them and although many thought she would never find a husband or was too 'old-fashioned' to keep a boyfriend, most of those who got to know her well admired her, none more so than Noah. Indeed, all of Book Four is devoted to his courting, engagement and finally his marriage to Miss Wonderful, the impeccable Sunita. Let his own words taken from his diary for these years tell their tale:

Love was more distant from my mind than Hell is from Heaven when I decided to go to Crete for a summer yoga course in the 1980s; holidays for me were never a matter of sun, sand and sex and certainly never ever an excuse for binge-drinking, girl-chasing or coming home suffering from severe sunburn. No; free-time had to be spent wisely and that meant doing a course of some description; art lessons, a language course, visits to museums and galleries, or guided visits to historical cities. I always wanted to return home a 'better, more cultured human being' and thus be a better citizen, colleague, neighbour, friend or lover.

After an intensive two-weeks yoga course I always went home feeling like a million dollars; participants in such courses will all say the same thing. Contact with those who shared my enthusiasms, love of yoga, vegetarianism, leading a socially useful life, wishing to leave the world a 'better place' than when born into it, helped me to keep positive and forge my own path through this 'vale of tears'. And so when I met Sunita one evening at supper, in the open-air dining area under starlight and within earshot of the sea-waves, that sense of well-being magnified. She was a 'head-turner' and she knew it but she kept herself to herself and never was one to show off, make a fuss, seek the limelight or 'gossip'. On the contrary, she was outwardly shy, self-effacing, considerate and always wore a simple, pleasant smile that revealed an honest soul. In brief, she was ideal company, radiated warmth and compassion and so she was popular; I was not surprised that I gravitated towards her when, on the evening in question, I saw her eating alone. And it was that simple fact that surprised me. Perhaps she was waiting for someone, who knows, but I didn't care, so I sat at her table on what would have been my fifth evening in south-west Crete.

We spent a good three hours together and clearly enjoyed each other's company; given that we were both graduates and shared a deep interest in yoga, vegetarianism, in travel and in other cultures and languages, this was to be expected. She had preferred Pilates to Tai Chi but agreed to join me next afternoon for the class in Tai Chi; she attended the 6–8 am yoga session whereas my course ran from 8–30—10–30 followed by brunch at noon; afternoons were free although there were organised swimming lessons, creative arts and craft classes, even rock-climbing for beginners. That said, many participants preferred to find a parasol and read a book on yoga, or a novel while sipping soda overlooking the sea waiting for the early evening classes in yoga, Tai Chi or Pilates. It was an ideal location: the sun and calm seas were guaranteed, the local 'taverns' overlooked the beach with its silk, stone-free sand, a gentle breeze was enough to take the sting out of the hot air. The 'yoga-beach' as the locals called it, was never crowded with rowdy holiday-makers who, in Heraklion and elsewhere on the island, overdrank, turned lobster-red and stayed up until the early hours of the morning waking up at noon or later, desperate for pain-killers!

Professional yoga tutors seem to choose 'off-the-beaten-track' locations and where we stayed proved the point. The locals would come at weekends and have their picnics and swims and beach walks or a stint in a paddle-boat with their families and then return home at sunset. Whether they came to the site outside the summer season I never asked; they kept themselves to themselves, seemingly unaware of the life-transforming power of yoga, meditation, Pilates and Tai Chi. But I knew what yoga did for my well-being and so I never missed one session, nor did Sunita. In a very short time, she and I became an 'item' and met every evening for supper together.

She told me some strange facts about her childhood. She often had vivid dreams and 'visions' and remembers in particular one night, when a mega-violent storm raged outside her bedroom window, being told in a dream that we were all 'half-dead angels' *and that was* 'not good' *for humanity! She was urged to* 'wake up and become a fully live angel and help others to do the same!' *It was a message that she would never ever forget. There were other dreams with other messages but the one mentioned had made the greatest impression on her. According to the Met Office, the storm that night cost the nation millions of pounds in damages. Inexplicably, her parents' house was the only house in her neighbourhood not to suffer any damage; not one broken or fallen roof-tile, not one cracked window-pane or flagstone, not even one broken branch from the several mature trees that surrounded the back of the house overlooking the garden. Everything inside and outside was left picture-perfect. Every blade of grass, every tiny plant, plant-pot and vulnerable petal, every twig on the large hedge that bordered the garden and even the clothes-line that was heavy with washing had been left unscathed. Reporters were quick to spot the anomaly and descended upon her 'space' eager for a scoop with or without possible explanations. Architects, town-planners and even two members of the 'Diviner's Association' came to inspect the premises but all left none the wiser. The beleaguered insurance company (it was the same company that insured all the homes in the area) sent its own surveyor to discover why Sunita's parents' house had remained intact and concluded that it* 'lay on a sacred ley-line linked to a distant tectonic plate'! *Sunita wisely said nothing about her dream, mention of which would have given local, national and international reporters a field-day, given that gossip, rumour and speculation govern their newspapers. And yet, honesty-loving Sunita wanted very much to divulge the truth – and the truth for her was,* 'celestial forces had knowingly protected her home and its contents' – *but such claims could easily have landed her in the mental wing of the local hospital or in the nearest asylum! And so she said nothing of what she knew; instead, she agreed with everybody else who claimed it must have been the work of fate, an 'act of God' and that simple phrase worked its magic. But it should be mentioned that every household in her neighbourhood discounted the 'act of God' clause when it came to their claims for damages to their properties! And the insurance company, after protracted court proceedings and with the greatest reluctance imaginable, eventually paid up, only to increase premiums six months later by a cruel 10 per cent.*

But the miracle of 'damage-free property' after the worst storm in living memory was less important to Sunita than the fact, which she confessed to Noah, that she didn't really know what was actually meant by the term 'half-dead angels', or how she could become a 'fully-live angel'? Would he be able to help her find the true meaning of the message because it was a message she clearly heard and vividly remembered? Noah naturally wanted to help, but he was no genie with a lamp or the owner of a magic carpet and calmly promised to do whatever he could because he 'loved to solve riddles' *and wished* 'he'd been born the fourth Magi, the fourth Wise Man who brought specific gifts to the infant Jesus'. *Sunita smiled hearing this allusion to an ancient event, but she was no nearer the answer she sought. But she was a patient soul and knew how to bide her time.*

She then went on to admit that she was able to 'hear the ticking of a watch with two or sometimes three rooms between her and the watch!' *If a fly, ladybird, butterfly or any similar-winged insect landed on the table in a room she was in, she felt a dull thud in both ears! When out walking in the countryside, she would sometimes put her ears to the ground and would immediately know if horses, cows or sheep (and how many!) were in the vicinity. Once or twice, she remembers being able to see through hills and mountains and on occasion, 'saw' people's thoughts. But as she got older, these things happened less and less; maybe for the better, but she still had very good hearing and put it down to early meditation practice with her parents. But she also 'confessed' to Noah that she never spoke to her parents about such experiences; she had no wish to be thought of as a freak or weirdo needing* 'therapy for having such uncommon gifts'. *No: she learned how to live with such assets and somehow coped. But out of all these happenings, she firmly believed that the instruction to wake up and become a 'fully live angel' was the most urgent. For, in her daily life, she was convinced that humanity had lost its way, had somehow lost contact with its own 'spiritual nature' and that, in many cases, had sunk to the level of the beast.* 'How else,' *she would ask herself,* 'could man create so many forms of torture, concentration camps, gas chambers, nuclear bombs, chemical warfare and allow most of mankind to live in poverty?' *She had no real wish to mention such serious matters while on holiday but neither could she forget that in that same dream she had been told to 'wake up and help others to do the same'! And when Noah mentioned, half-jokingly, that* 'our world is a vale of tears', *she immediately agreed and then asked him this*: 'If the world is so, how can we accept it as such, and still try to live fulfilled and meaningful lives, for deep down we all want to be happy, not miserable, right?'

Noah had to agree, saying, 'We have to discover the things we need to do to become happy, and stop doing the things we know that make us unhappy. For we have choices, no matter the circumstances. After all, in this we are all in the same boat. We all have to face pain, frustration, disappointment and the loss of things we love as well as the failure to get what we want. We all have to experience growing up and the competition that society throws at us, at home, school and at work; and if we live long enough, we all have to face old age and the infirmities it brings, the ever-presence and reality of death and eventually say goodbye to those we love and know, relatives, friends, neighbours and work colleagues, every single one. For that is the reality of human experience on a daily basis; in a nutshell, life as we know it incorporates suffering, and the sooner we accept that as fact, the better. Now that is easily said but to achieve that acceptance requires' – and here Noah looked at Sunita straight into her eyes – 'a degree of understanding of what it is to be human'.

I could feel that Sunita agreed; she readily saw the sense of what I had been saying and that made me glad. For what I had said I believed was true: every human being that lives 'three-score and ten and more', cannot escape life's problems that are built into existence. In sum, everything that is born must die. We all live in an unstable world where nothing remains the same for long. Impermanence is the hall-mark of our experiences on planet earth; lasting happiness is a dream. The common experience of everyday life tells us that nothing endures, happiness is always bracketed by dissatisfaction, regrets, disappointments, mistakes and failures. Hearing such 'facts-of-life' awakened in Sunita something she had always known, a home-truth acquired in former lives. I even wondered if she saw in me a soul-mate, or in my more imaginative moments, someone who aspired to become a 'fully live angel', a semi-divine entity?

When the holiday was over we kept up contact via e-mails, mobiles and texting. Bristol to Chorley is no marathon and so, occasionally, we would meet up for Sunday lunch and put the world to rights. But then, inevitably, it was time to meet her parents, a momentous event that took place the following February, the 14th, St Valentines, a date chosen by her mother. But it was not a romantic dinner just for two; far from it. We all went to a local Indian restaurant where the family was well-known and liked. With Sunita present, nothing would get too serious or unpleasant, so I thought, but I was mistaken: in my diary entry for the occasion I called it a 'mini Inquisition'.

CHAPTER 6

Were my intentions honourable? What was my family background? Had I ever been engaged or even married? What were my future plans, job-wise? Was I a home-owner? Did I smoke or have any secret vices such as gambling, alcohol, excessive playing of video-games, pornography, so-called recreational drugs?

I kept my cool because none of such vices applied to me in any shape or form; in brief they held no appeal to me, whatsoever. I spoke a little of my early home-life and of my stint in a boarding school and that, yes, I was a home-owner and that, as regards my future plans, job-wise, I hoped to join the Inspectorate. Sunita told them that my intentions were 'very honourable' and by that they knew she was still a virgin! By the time dessert was served, everybody seemed to be in a good mood. Not until one week later did Sunita let it be known that her parents thought I was a 'suitable male-friend' and so they both felt relieved. Her mother had read and heard of so many broken relationships, separations, divorces, ugly law-suits, fights about custody of children that she couldn't help but worry herself sick, have sleepless nights and very recently and just prior to my visit, had to resort to pain-killers and sleeping pills.

Her father, however, was much more relaxed about our 'relationship'; he was rather happy that she had met an educated Englishman who had a worthwhile profession and a rather noble 'set of attitudes' that demanded respect, if not praise. He very *much wanted to see grand-children mainly because he had been the only child, had never seen his grandparents, had one uncle who, due to chronic asthma and severe diabetes, lived in a private nursing home near York. There were also two aunts, twins, who lived in Truro and who spent their days (both were long retired), working in charity shops and at weekends, visiting the 'lonely sick' in hospitals; apparently in the south-west of England there are many widows, widowers and singletons who have no one to visit them. Both women had worked almost forty years in the prison service and now they wanted to keep themselves to themselves. As a result, Sunita's amiable father, Ralph, got the odd 'phone-call or e-mail and birthday card. Ralph had very few relatives and so his 'family life' revolved around his wife's extended family and he really enjoyed that; his home was like a small hotel, guests were coming and going all the time, and the most recent had been Sunita accompanied by clean-living, God-fearing, yoga-disciplined Noah.*

Noah was relieved that her parents had given him the thumbs up; both he and his 'fine catch of a girlfriend' knew he deserved their full approval. They kept working hard and began to budget rather than save but it came to the same thing; to Sunita, if things really took off between them – and she secretly hoped it would – she knew that Noah was a proud home-owner and she was more than willing to move to Chorley. For Noah, he knew in his bones that he had met a true diamond and soon began to hear the seductive sound of not so distant wedding-bells. And that is what happened the following August but not before their annual 'yoga pilgrimage' to Crete for their favourite yoga course. Luckily but deserved, Sunita found a well-paid post working in a very prestigious law firm (in its international wing) in nearby Preston and proved to be very popular; she also joined the local Rambler's association and settled into what seemed an idyllic lifestyle; both were over the proverbial moon and couldn't believe their good fortune. In time, Sunita dabbled in both Irish and clog dancing that were popular in the region and soon made rapid progress. What more could she want? Noah asked himself the same question and drew a blank. But an answer was already 'in the air'.

More than anything else, Sunita's parents, especially mother, wanted grandchildren; they wanted to become doting grandparents and thus enjoy what remained to them of what they saw as the 'miracle and mystery of human life'. Both Sunita and I knew what her parents wanted and looked forward to, but other matters had also to be considered. Our new jobs in a relatively new location meant a great deal to career-minded professionals in the first throes of 'true love'. Although against her 'principles', Sunita was on the pill; at this point in our marriage, she showed no interest in 'breeding as giving further purpose to her life'. We both had no desire to be saddled with 'early parenthood' and had agreed to wait until her early thirties before adding to the world's population. That was our plan and we stuck to it until the 'accident' that changed everything. Looking forward to our third Christmas together, Sunita, somewhat nervously it must be said, let it be known she was pregnant! Later scans showed she was pregnant with twin-boys!

At first, we were both shell-shocked, or that, at least it was how it felt. Neither of us knew what to say. Had she come off the pill without telling me? Doubts, questions, fears, worries, surprise and disbelief followed in quick succession leading, at first to confusion, and then, when reality set in, to acceptance.

The fact of the matter was clear to all: Sunita was to become a mother and me a father. And that simple truth was something her parents had long been waiting to hear and to celebrate and they did. In time, we, as parents-to-be, very much looked forward to an event that we both had tried hard to prevent. We turned the spare-room into a cot room and had it decorated and furnished for the new arrivals. From tests and scans, the birth was predicted to fall on full moon the following May. Names had already been chosen for the twin boys; Mahinda and Rahula. When Sunita went to hospital for a routine delivery, she suddenly suffered severe convulsions and fell into a deep coma and never recovered; she died from what was called 'eclampsia'!

Doctors, nurses, consultants, other expectant mothers in the same ward and high-ranking NHS advisers were left in total shock. No one could explain the tragedy, least of all her parents. I was absolutely devastated and cried non-stop for one whole week until my eyes wept blood. The obligatory inquest offered no other explanation; medical authorities accepted the cause of death as eclampsia, a condition that affects pregnant women, although Sunita's case was the first of its occurrence in the local hospital. The cremation service that followed ten days after her death was a gloom-laden event; grief-stricken parents, relatives, friends and colleagues formed a small army of mourners clutching their damp handkerchiefs unable to say a word. In the wake that followed the cremation, very little was eaten or drunk; after all, no words could change what had happened, we all were aware of that and so time passed painfully slowly for each of us. I wanted to be left in peace and grieve alone at home. And that is what I did. Her unexpected and sudden death compelled me to reconsider my life and what had been my life's goals. Destiny had dealt me such a blow that there were moments when I felt suicidal. I couldn't eat, think straight, sleep at night or function as a normal human being. Something had to give.

If we can accept what was written in Book Three of the diaries and we have no real reason not to, it is claimed that one month after the cremation, when it was full-moon, Sunita 'appeared' to Noah in his sleep and told him that she was now with 'fully-alive angels' in an ante-chamber of Heaven and was happy and at peace! She had met, and made friends with, wonderful people who worked solely for the welfare of humanity. But all of them, in time, including herself, would return to Planet Earth and resume their individual quest to seek 'release from decay and death for ever and thus break the cycle of rebirth'. She continued thus:

'More I'm not allowed to say, whether of the spacious realms you call Heaven or what we do here although we are continually active but in ways beyond no human being can imagine. But I do have a special message for you and that's why I have come to you tonight. You can't have forgotten the vivid dream I once told you about when I mentioned that humanity is made up of 'half-dead angels' and that I was asked to change that and lead others to become 'fully live angels'. That very request I now pass on to you. You have the knowledge and skill to achieve that in others. It's no easy undertaking, but we up here are all here to help you. Trust me in this; all of us in the 'star-world' will be at your side. No work at the present time is more urgent.'

As Casey read these words, he felt a presence in the room, but he was not afraid or startled and certainly was not hallucinating as some of his friends would claim. In his imagination, he could hear them: *"Come on, Casey, you're delusional. You've had a pint too many and that's made you fantasize! Put what you're reading down and go and get a real book, a comic, anything, but don't expect us to fall for fairy tale stuff about visions and conversations with the dead!"*

And yes, they had a point; what they laughed at made logical sense. That said, Casey knew that a presence was near-by and nothing could make him change his mind. Noah's Spiritualist friends would support his claim; they know that souls or spirits that have very recently 'moved on' very often linger, and many do appear to their most beloved ones in dreams. Paranormal literature is full of such 'ghostly' events and although a good number of leading scientists and psychologists accept them as bona-fide, the public at large discount such claims as fairy-stories or the products of deranged minds. Casey, however, does not belong to the 'public at large'; he readily accepted what the diary claimed and read on with growing curiosity. For, as yet, Sunita had not finished:

'For you to show others the ancient path to lasting happiness, the 'Heaven' or 'The Promised Land' that all religions talk about, you'll need extra-terrestrial help; in brief, you'll need special training. With such help, you'll be able to teach others the purpose of life and in so doing make this world a better place. Could there be a greater, or more noble task than this? No, there isn't! You know that and I know that, but I also know that you were born to do it. Yet, because of the enormity of the mission – for that is what it is – we have searched the globe to find you other pure-hearted souls to accompany you. We have found five suitable candidates, one from each continent but as yet nothing has been finalised and so, for the time being, you'll have to work 'alone' but you can never be 'alone' in this task. You have us!'

At this point, Casey stopped reading; he had to, so overwhelmed did he feel at the immensity of the task she had set Noah. But there was much more to make him pause. Her 'death', her appearance in a dream-like sequence, her extraordinary request to Noah, were all 'things' no one who had begun reading the note-pads could ever have imagined or envisaged! He even began to doubt what he was reading and sensed that any future reader, who had got this far, would throw the book, the novel, call it what you will, high into the air or into a fire if one was near-by, and rush away in disgust or in anger. Yet, behind all such thoughts of doubts and outrageous, impossible requests, he could not lose sight of Sunita's honesty or of Noah's integrity and so he somehow managed to keep his cool and went on reading.

'To assist you in your mission, I have brought you a special gift. You'll find it on the kitchen table. Go there after I have said what I've been sent to say. But always remember, if you ever feel unable to continue, call out my name and I'll appear on the instant. That's a promise made in Heaven! We all wish you well on your journey through this 'vale of tears' as you used to say, and that's a valid description because all human experience is subject to constant change, for nothing endures. This year's birds don't live in last year's nests! The journey ahead of you, if you accept the challenge, will be an adventure beyond all imagination; a journey in which no two days can ever be the same. Blessings from above!'

In what seemed a super-subtle shower of stardust, she disappeared as suddenly as she had arrived. Noah was left in disbelief; he was by now wide-awake and so got up and made his way to the table in the kitchen on which he found a lotus-flower and a note. He picked up the note that said:

*'If you truly want to know why you were born and what life is for and what lies beyond life on Earth, contact, using this mantra…
(a name and address in Benares, in northern India, followed).*

'The lotus flower is your "passport" to persons, places and structures that very few on Earth know about, but they exist, and have existed since the dawn of time. It also serves as a map that shows secret routes (inter-stellar and subterranean) that you may have to use from time to time. It's self-luminous, so you can 'read' it anywhere, anytime. This wonderful flower grows in the evergreen gardens that surround the immortal mystery schools which, if you agree to the mission, will have to attend. The flower before you can never wither or die; it is both indestructible and 'invisible' to every human eye except yours. It can never be lost, stolen, copied or reproduced. Your journey – if you agree to the undertaking – *begins in three months from today and that day is the first full moon in September.*

'I know that you will decide to do this, not for me, not for you, but for the welfare of humanity. We both know the world is at a perilous crossroads; wars, especially in the 20th century, famines, earthquakes, viral-diseases, climate change and probably the worst of all, man's relentless inhumanity to man, characterise the present age. Sadly, we do not seem to learn from the past.

'Life, of itself, necessarily incorporates suffering, so why do human beings add to it? Your efforts will go towards the creation of a better world; think of those born today and of those countless millions yet to be born. Do they not deserve a better, more humane legacy from those that went before them? You know they do, so make it happen! Coraggio!'

CHAPTER 7

Wow! What a meeting with someone who now belonged to the 'living dead' because Sunita had been cremated – he had seen it take place – but she was no longer 'dead'. If she were, how could she re-appear at will and talk so naturally as if nothing had ever happened to her? He felt privileged; he had just spoken to his 'wife' who was alive and well and active on another astral plane. More to the point was that she had put him in contact with a celestial being who was living in Benares and only a mantra sound-wave away!

At this point, Casey stopped reading; he needed time to digest such an amount of extraordinary dialogue that, in its detail, defied belief. He was made to think back to Sunita's account of that violent storm that occurred in her childhood and had ravaged almost everything in sight in her neighbourhood except for her parents' home and garden in which, so she claims, not 'one twig or blade of grass' had been touched! And it was that very night when, in her dream, she was told to 'wake up' and become a 'fully live angel'. But fate intervened and called her away to an antechamber of Heaven where she found peace and harmony and now works with others 'for the welfare of the world'.

Not said until now, the unseen narrator has been informed – and allowed to tell readers – that Sunita's current colleagues in their shared celestial home are the very ones who made sure her parents' home was left intact and undamaged in that storm all those years ago. Casey also learns of this and accepts it willingly, but he still needs to time to consider what he has been reading. And if that is true for him, what about the reader, too? In brief, has not too much been said too quickly? For a start, what would any reader make of Sunita's alleged apparition and subsequent conversation with Noah, 'inviting' him to contact an ascended master for a sacred mission? For all such details are given: add to them the claim that the lotus-flower is both 'indestructible and invisible' and had been left by Sunita on the kitchen-table – an extraordinary, extra-terrestrial gift – to be used to complete a quest that had been shown to her in a dream long ago, a dream as real as any experience of hers while physically 'awake'.

It is all an enigma, a real puzzle and every bit as mysterious as Sunita's tragic demise that left Noah devastated, her parents heart-broken and her law-firm colleagues speechless. That said, Casey is aware – as is every reader of this text – that he has to come to terms with Sunita's 'moving on'. She no longer lives on Earth, her cremation is proof of that, but can he – can we? – accept that she's still alive but on a different astral level? Noah has no doubt whatsoever and is convinced that she does. Her unexpected appearance and her 'startling' message with its untold implications for him are no figments of the imagination, the stuff of 'fairy-tales', as Noah's old friends would argue. No; for him she lives on and so does her mission, too. Besides, his extensive reading of various literatures has taught him that the unexpected occurs far more often than is generally believed and not just in major sporting events; results in football, horseracing, bingo and lotto prove this beyond all doubt.

No one could have possibly foreseen or imagined Sunita's tragic death from eclampsia, but it occurred and compelled a distraught Noah to re-evaluate his life and his priorities. But then, how many young widowers are offered the amazing invitation to attend ancient mystery schools so as to be able to guide humanity to a level of awareness and achievement that have always been there for human beings but forgotten, even abandoned for other, far less important things? After all, Casey thought to himself, how did it come about that Lucifer, allegedly the most brilliant of all intelligent creatures, became so insane that he willed to be greater than his creator? Adam may have been deceived, but who deceived Lucifer? Bearing such questions in mind, the reader is reminded that behind Noah's mission lies the unexpressed wish for a Utopia on Planet Earth, possibly to make the known dream of a 'heaven on earth' a reality?

And for such a dream to become true, the world certainly needed the assistance of an ascended master. Sunita's mention of such a figure living currently in Benares took Casey by surprise. And so he was curious to see Noah's response to such an amazing offer. For Casey had read and had accepted that Christ had attended such esoteric schools in the hidden years between twelve and thirty, years during which he underwent special training so as to prepare him for his world-changing mission.

Everyone alive could see that living in today's world meant facing difficulties, strife, suffering, injustice, pain and disease. Casey didn't have to be told of the dangerous crossroads humanity had reached. Life in the twentieth century had seen two World Wars (he viewed WW2 as a continuation of WW1); the Spanish Civil War; the Great Depression; the invasion of Tibet; the social revolutions in China, Russia and Cuba; the growth of cancer; the outbreak of AIDS and so on, and what was desperately needed was a guideline, knowledge (esoteric or not), an authoritative voice to lead humanity forward and upward. Compassion for others, regardless of colour, creed, social background, education or one's income, had to become the catalyst for a crusade of moral and social reform launched by the 'highest' minds around. Casey agreed that such a programme was absolutely necessary. But the question was how to instigate it and with what?

What happens next is vividly recorded by Noah in his Fourth notepad:

It was gone midnight when most good souls were fast asleep that I sounded the sacred mantra. Within seconds, I saw an image of a man wearing what seemed to be a Roman senator's toga; on his feet were leather sandals made from camel-skin and highly polished. As if in conversation via Skype, he began as follows:

'My dear friend Noah. My celestial name is Nabi *and I am here to bring you a message. Firstly, let me say, I know everything about you and have been waiting for this moment since before your first memory. For I know your previous births and what it is that has brought you to me, here and now. For nothing is an accident; indeed, everything that happens, falls under eternal laws, one of which is the Law of Cause and Effect. Whatever you do in life will have an effect on someone or on something and that will come to light sooner or later. Simply put, what you have done in previous lives has led you to me, just as it had led you to Sunita.*

'The lotus flower Sunita left for you comes from me; it is a mystical heirloom. I used its powers aeons ago, as did others before and after me. It can be worn around your neck held by a thread, invisible to others, but not to you. As Sunita has already explained, it is invisible, indestructible, can never be lost or stolen. It is now yours, given to assist you in your task, that is, if you accept the challenge. *Let me quickly add this: I already know your response and that precisely is why I am here now before you.*

'I also know that you are wondering, "Why me? Why Noah Azrael Salmon? What have I done in previous lives to deserve this opportunity?"

'And so let me say something of birth and rebirth for nothing exists on its own but always has come from earlier circumstances; we can call this the Law of Causality and operates throughout every life, the present as well as all past lives.

'Let me begin by telling you that the pattern of the heavens at the moment of birth is a blueprint of how one's life will unfold. Furthermore, the life to be led by any individual can be interpreted by the trained astrologer which I am. Deep study of the constellations, the signs of the zodiac and of how the planets influence human life belong to astrology that has formed part of man's understanding from prehistoric times. Ancient astronaut theorists rightly claim that such knowledge was originally brought to your Planet Earth by the 'star-people', teachers from outer space whose task it was to care for and educate infant humanity. I am one of such star-people and evidence of our teaching is to be found in the design of ancient monuments such as Stonehenge, the pyramids in Egypt, the Ajanta caves in India and in Petra, and elsewhere, but also in ancient myths and legends. The truths about such myths, monuments and symbolism, but especially about the great Laws of Creation, will be conveyed to you in esoteric schools that are found on all five continents. Fortunately for you, humanity is awakening to the reality of what you call ETs and UFOs; the possibility of life on other planets is discussed openly and the gradual release of government classified secret documents that focus on 'aliens' has made humanity more receptive to our presence even though we live so many light years away from Planet Earth. But our

technology is such that our spacecraft can reach Earth in a matter of 'Earthly hours'.

'"But why me, Noah Azrael Salmon?" I hear you repeat inside your head. And the question is to be expected. There exists in life a little-known law, the 'law of opportunity *'; it enables each person born on Earth (and elsewhere) to reveal and develop those gifts of mind and spirit that come with a specific birth. Such gifts you have and this now is your opportunity to use them to help others to develop their 'specific gifts' for humanity's greatest good. Such an aim runs counter to the common pursuit of personal advantage or self-interest that everyone seems to follow. You have an opportunity to change that trend which very often brings home nothing but unprofitable scars!*

That said, I have to put this question before you, here and now: Are you willing to accept the challenge, the greatest you will ever face, and carry out the required training in one of our esoteric schools of mystery?'

Although I felt overwhelmed, knowing that my new mentor seemed to know everything about me put me at ease; he was aware my life was at a crossroads and that out of my love for Sunita I was 'ready' to undertake the wholly unexpected and carry her mission forward. For in my heart of hearts, I knew that birth and rebirth had a purpose, that existence did not begin and stop at the physical and that there was much more behind the scenes and events of everyday life that we all commonly see and experience. Clearly, a power existed, an organising power that was somehow functioning and whose purpose it was to bring humanity to a level over and above the level of 'homo sapiens', above the level of the angelic orders to a state that some call 'nirvana', heavenly bliss, the seventh heaven, paradise itself.

Whether my view of such a purpose was correct or that I had a part to play in it, I couldn't say with certainty, but I felt it, intuitively. That said, what had I to lose when at my side stood a divine being, one of the 'star-people', an ascended master who had been patiently waiting for me, allegedly since before my current birth, to answer this one question?

From deep within my being – from a place that had always been there life after life but until my previous life inaccessible – I heard a voice that rang out clearer than any newly tuned cathedral bell, saying, 'Yes! I accept! I accept!' And as I said this, I felt an opening of my heart and saw with my 'inner eye' my aura – that I'd been told everybody has but is rarely seen – that began to radiate light that soon turned into a halo, the sign of peace that brings healing and comfort to others.

'Your decision fills me with joy and will be written in the eternal Tablet of Destinies *kept by the four archangels who record all truly sacrificial actions, for only such actions change the world for the better. We up here will mark this day as your real birthday. So now go ahead and apply for a sabbatical and prepare yourself for the most rigorous physical and mental training possible. Nothing less will allow you to carry out a mission hardly any other soul on Earth knows about; the training will also teach you how to be in constant telepathic contact with me. You have my blessing and support and the support of Sunita and her friends who make up the 'living dead' and live in one of Heaven's countless antechambers that are protected by the rulers of the zodiac. Such chambers are sealed off from all poisons and pollutants that your planet continuously discharges. May I just add that it's the function of a good number of ETs to neutralize such pollution that, if left untreated, would contaminate other planets in your solar system. I will be in touch with you sooner*

than you think with details about your 'training' in one of the several sacred schools of mystery that have always existed.'

And with that, the ascended master and prophet named Nabi merged into the ether and was gone. Wide-awake and receptive, I had no wish to return to my bed so I spent 'quiet time' pondering on both Sunita's and my new teacher's words. As I did so, I could feel around my neck the tiny 'flower-from-heaven' gift that Sunita had left for me on the kitchen table and which, no doubt, ethereal Nabi had put on me, but unseen and unfelt, during our conversation. Such beings often play that sort of trick; it keeps us all on our toes for such tricks always have a purpose. It dawned on me that this heavenly heirloom was to be my coat-of-arms. Every warrior worthy of the name that we can read about in literatures from around the world always had his shield or emblem; but no warrior had ever fought the wars that lay ahead of me. I had entered an arena that was timeless, universal, constantly changing and, at the moment of entry, unknown, full of dangers, bristling with obstacles and filled with both 'light and dark forces'. I had entered a stadium where very few had been before me, that stadium of the human spirit where untold treasures lay: true freedom, the knowledge that lay beyond understanding, eternal peace, everlasting bliss and immortality.

Nothing less was the reward on offer, not just for me, but for all men everywhere, but especially for those yet to be born. We have all read of the extraordinary acts of sacrifice, prowess, skill and human endurance achieved by others before us. Even those who have won Olympic gold medals in modern times have had to show unbelievable commitment, sacrifice, endurance and patience, but all such admirable human qualities fade fast when compared to the battles that lay ahead of me to obtain the greatest prize of all; immortality, and thus join the muses, the gods on ancient and indestructible Mount Olympus…

At this point, Casey intervenes, telling us that we cannot overestimate the undertaking Noah has so nobly accepted on behalf of a sick and struggling mankind in the third millennium. If ever anyone born human needed and deserved our every support, praise, admiration and prayers, surely it would have to be Noah Azrael Salmon who, in terms of wealth, social status, titles and basic income was a relative nobody, another 'one of us', a simple soul seeking a simple, productive life, willing to enjoy life's pleasures and avoid Nature's dangers and in due time, leave the world a better place than when he first entered it.

Casey was aware that Noah's battle would also be a battle against our accepted finite limitations of perspective, because life as we know it would not be life without such, but neither could life be what it could be if we were satisfied with them. Noah had been 'chosen' to help create a new world, a new mentality, a new breed of being, able to live intergalactic life and willing to receive help from our extra-terrestrial friends with their advanced technologies? Had Nabi already told Sunita of Noah's momentous decision, one that Nabi had known since before Noah's first memory? Casey felt certain he had and so he smiled, unaware that Sunita and her 'living-dead' colleagues were also smiling with him in an antechamber somewhere not far away in the 'star-world'.

CHAPTER 8

Casey's thoughts continued into what had now become chapter four of his readings of Noah's notepads. He was convinced that the sterling character we now all know as Noah Salmon, he who had been granted a sabbatical leave during which he was to carry out an unheard-of mission far greater than any of those carried out by legendary medieval knights of old, or even by Spain's indomitable knight-errant, Don Quixote; neither was, nor could be, the *same* Mr Noah Salmon who, not that long ago, had functioned as a maths teacher in a sixth form college in NW England. Having recently lost his loving wife, partner, support and best friend, he was now a reluctant widower who, through a series of bizarre events and circumstances, had been compelled to reflect on his life, past and future, but it was the future that dominated his thoughts. And then, dramatically and overnight, he'd become a 'man with a mission', a mission that thereafter was to define his very existence on Planet Earth until his final breath.

The ordeal that he was to undertake was so vast in scope and so critical for the future welfare of mankind – and this is said without one iota of exaggeration – that even mighty Hercules would have feared for his life and Krypton-born megastar Superman tremble for his sanity! How could any human achieve what inoffensive, mild-mannered and yoga-loving Noah had willingly agreed to undertake? Casey is as curious as we are to find out what happened next? After all, we all know that so much in life is uncertain and fraught with peril. So, how does Noah react to his encounter with his mentor and guide? The entry in his diary tells us all:

No human could ever be the same after a meeting with a divine being who, seemingly, knew more about me than I did about myself! Yet the fact that he did know all about me reassured me much more than I can put into words. Psychologists tell us that fear of isolation is innate in all men and women and indeed, there were moments after Sunita's passing that I felt alone, abandoned, even lost. But no longer; Nabi had given me a task that had arisen as a by-product of the little-known 'law of opportunity', *a law that could and would transform my life on Planet Earth forever. That is what I believed and that belief gave power to my overall purpose which was to 'awaken and instil in others' an awareness of our full human potential. Achieving this would lead to the state of living life as a 'fully alive angel', a plane of existence first introduced to me by Sunita.*

The task set fascinated me as much as my imminent attendance in a sacred School of Mystery, no matter where! After all, everyone's true happiness – and that was integral to the goal set – consists solely in the enjoyment of the good, true and beautiful. How many times Sunita and I had come to that very viewpoint I can't say, but very many. And now, as I embarked on a journey into the unknown, she was with me, for I was continuing a mission delivered to her in a dream that was not really a dream but something real on another astral plane well-known to theologians and philosophers, moralists and artists. Tradition holds that there are nine grades of such creatures in the celestial hierarchy, but in Sunita's 'dream' nothing was mentioned about such grades or such a hierarchy. To become such a 'being' appeared to me as the next feasible step in human evolution and I felt privileged to help bring it about. After Sunita's 'appearances' to me and then after my initial 'contact' with Master Nabi, I had no doubt that the message, the mission and goal were realities within arm's length. But wait! Just pause and consider for a moment what I have just said! The mission, to help and show mankind how to evolve and attain the next stage or grade in evolution, the status of 'angel-hood', were 'realities within arm's length'!

To attain that wondrous 'grade' of being that, in time, would lead to true happiness on Earth would require a massive transformation in our thinking, behaviour and values, our moral values. For, is it not true, that only by love of virtue do men attain happiness? And it goes without saying that I saw my mission not only as virtuous but also as the ladder to attain the happiness all men seek. Nabi would never allow a disciple or student of his to be involved in anything less!

The school authorities reluctantly let me go for they knew that I was good at my job, got on well with colleagues and had improved pupils' grades in GCSE exams. But they also knew that a year passes quickly and that they had my written promise, duly signed and dated, of my return. As mentioned, my master, from this point on called Nabi, contacted me with details of a school in Upper Egypt. I spent three months there and a further three months in a similar school in the province of Bihar, in India. What I saw, experienced and was taught in both schools will be revealed in due course but here and now, at this stage in my journal, is best left undiscussed. This may upset some readers and I apologise, but my motive for the delay is genuine. For I feel that many, if not most, readers would find it difficult to digest and grasp what was taught. Even up to this point have I not *mentioned things, events, encounters that will have stretched most readers' powers of acceptance and belief to the limit? The miracle of Sunita's parents' home that was the only house in the entire neighbourhood not to suffer any damage whatsoever from one of the worst storms in living memory; the appearance of Sunita to me shortly after her 'passing' with her special request; the introduction to Nabi, an ascended master, who became my tutor and mentor and with whom I was to be in constant communication via telepathy; the 'living dead' who live in one of the countless antechambers of Heaven and who work tirelessly for the well-being of mankind. Such revelations to my curious and friendly readers have been more than enough to 'swallow' in the opening chapters. And so the soul-stirring events that took place in the ancient mystery schools are best left to later. Trust me on this!*

But suffice to say that not one moment of my precious time in such schools was wasted. Sacred mantras, symbols and texts were given to me to love and learn by heart. I am free to say that everything I did and saw I wrote in Diary Five but with the use of 'invisible ink'; without the magic code, drawn from an ancient Akkadian text, the diary remains a blank and so for now, you will all have to show patience. And that applies to any future biographer, too. For I have it on the best authority that biographers will want to write about me and my exploits! Nabi has assured me, however, that my stay in such schools and what I was taught in them will one day soon become 'public property', but safeguarded for posterity by the five, as yet unmentioned, souls who have been found and chosen to assist me and my work on Earth. And that day is not far off – indeed it is imminent – by virtue of this prophecy: 'Whenever,' said Nabi, 'materialism is rampant and misery overruns the world, Diary Five will come to light and enter the public domain.' His words were said with great solemnity and conviction. I had a very clear sense that that 'day of declaration', as I call it, is already upon us. All readers of this diary are urged to reflect on Nabi's words; his words are certainly material for any sequel to this text and will be of immense interest, delight and consolation to all future readers. I can say this because I know what I saw and what I did and what I was taught. And all of it was done with the noble intention of benefitting others, no matter who or where and, although on my return to my day-job I kept my secrets to myself without telling a soul of what really took place during my sabbatical, I was told to make a careful and accurate note of everything in a journal for 'those yet to be born human'. For now, however, the willing reader – and Casey – will have to move on to Diary Six.

CHAPTER 9

Sympathetic readers who have reached this far – and that's no mean achievement – will want to know what I did when I returned from my 'training in foreign fields'; for, as already mentioned at the opening of the previous chapter, the Noah Salmon who left his place of work did not return the same person even though my name and physical appearance hadn't changed. I kept to my promise and returned to my old post as assistant head of maths at the college in Chorley. But my focus was elsewhere; although a core subject and one I loved, maths no longer took centre-stage in my working life or in life in general. Clearly, I did the best for my pupils – and for my fellow teachers – until my early retirement, earlier than planned. The work to help others to realise their full potential and become 'fully live angels' took over; outwardly nothing had changed. I went to school, taught my classes, fulfilled my contractual duties and was a reliable colleague. But in every class taught, in every conversation spoken, in every meeting held, I never lost sight of my goal. Every subject in the school curriculum can be linked to what is our purpose and function as human beings; teaching offers us great opportunities and so, in my classes, I almost always found a moment to bring in 'real knowledge'. It took tact, patience and an alert mind but it seemed to work. I saw myself following the famous parable of the seed-thrower; I scattered good, fertile seeds not knowing when such seeds would come to flower or with whom.

In this way, I led a double-life; I was a secret double agent and thrived on the anonymity. No one except for my mentor, Nabi and Sunita with her colleagues among the 'living dead' really knew my true and noble agenda, an agenda that was more hidden than the Ark of the Covenant, the Holy Grail or the fabled land of Eldorado. I became a living James Bond character without the James Bond girlfriends, the fast cars, the amazing stunts and without the Star Wars gadgetry that 'wow' all of his fans, everywhere. But there was a difference; I was for real, not for make-believe. James Bond and his ilk create and live escapism; the greater the illusion, the more convincing the stunt, the better the entertainment and the more profits at the box-office. And we all admire and noisily applaud their skill as actors. Escapism in such films offers world-weary parents, the sick and disabled, the unemployed and the unemployable, the depressed and chronically ill, even the highly successful workaholics, a break from the harsh realities of the modern world. We all need time to stop clock-watching or meeting a dead-line, closing a lucrative business deal, passing an exam or making that extra dollar for the proverbial 'rainy day'. But I'd always sought something beyond sense enjoyment; if we are composed of mind, body and spirit, all three aspects have to be fed and watered. Nabi had given me true manna from heaven but with the express condition to pass it on to others, and for me, the 'others' were all those I met (and were yet to meet) in everyday life. And so when I took retirement – one year earlier than the norm – I saw the opportunity to widen my circle of 'others'; the vast reading public became my outlet and so it was that my diaries were to become public property. Overnight, I became a public servant. I was there to serve society's real needs and would do so in the truest sense of the term. My A4 notepads offered me a blank canvas to write something of lasting value that would help my fellow-man on our shared path through this vale of tears that ends in our physical decay and inescapable death. Nabi had told me long ago that my 'scribblings' would one day be found by 'a relative' and thus would be saved from 'decay, decomposition and all-pervading dust'! Nabi was well aware of what that meant to me; I heard him once call his toga 'an indestructible dust-jacket', a very appropriate term for an ascended master, one of the immortals. To know that all-invasive dust would not affect my 'meditations or philosophisings' strengthened my resolve, if that was at all possible. He was right because today's ways of storage (discs, memory sticks and cloudland) do not attract insatiable termites or insidious worms. My future lay in cloudland, both literally and figuratively. It's where I am now, perhaps?

At this stage in the diaries, there was a paragraph added written in the same calligraphic hand that began what Casey has come to consider as a mini-prologue to the diaries beginning with the sentence: *A question hangs over every life...*

Its contents caught Casey's keen eye. It reads as follows:

The night before my first day as a retired teacher of maths, I had a visitation from Nabi. Wearing the very same indestructible toga-garment as when we first met shortly after Sunita's death, he appeared to me in a cascade of midnight-blue light that lit up the lounge where I was reading a text on cosmology written by ancient astronaut theorists. I was wide awake and in control of my thoughts and senses. I say this because I need to emphasise that what 'happened' was no dream-sequence, mirage, or a hallucination provoked by magic mushrooms or something stronger. Nabi glowed in the penumbra of the lounge where I often read my favourite texts; he hadn't aged at all, not even one single nanosecond. In fact, nothing about him, his speech, clothes, aura, his indefinable charisma and magnetism, nothing about him was any different. It was as if the time between the two visits had never happened. I felt calm and protected. And then with a gracious smile, he spoke to me:

'My dear friend Noah, your true work now begins; retirement means you can now dedicate all your energies to the work you began all those years ago. We in the upper regions of what you call Heaven have watched your career progress and blossom and applaud the manner in which you were able to sow countless seeds to those who crossed your path. Some of those seeds have flowered and will continue to do so. But now you need to address the widest audience possible. Your innate love of wisdom and of literature has prepared you to compose texts that will be of great use to others in your world. What you have been taught in the schools of mystery has introduced you to the most uplifting of concepts and principles that underpin all worthwhile living. You must now use those same ideas and ideals in your writing so as to help others to seek and develop their human potential for it is vast, untapped and life-affirming, but all too often remains untouched. The result is that countless millions tend to lead unfulfilled lives, life after life. Knowing this, you can see how your 'work' from this moment onwards is both urgent and necessary.

But I know that writing, no matter the genre, is extremely competitive; texts that offer a different vision, a different menu from the diet of persecution, drug-abuse, domestic violence, mental illness, the misery of living in a dysfunctional family and so on rarely win literary competitions. Themes and characters that abound in dystopian texts, television soaps, kitchen-sink *dramas and billion dollar-costing escapist films seem to scoop everything; far too often, texts that show noble ideals, the perennial truths of the human condition or point to higher aims are dismissed as 'unrealistic, pie-in-the-sky, totally unmarketable, or even boring'. That being so, you'll have to write something that will immediately attract the attention of unwilling publishers, cautious editors, profit-seeking marketing men, touchy literary critics and, above all else, the attention of the reading public that is craving for a text that offers 'real medicine', real beer that soothes the spirit, delights the mind and cleanses the heart. I know you can write such a text and we all up here want to help you do just that.*

'Fiction is an immensely wide category but what readers tend to forget is that fiction, by definition, is not true but imaginary, unreal, in fact a pack of lies often presented as if genuine and authentic. And that's the rub because the contents of your work will be true: true to fact, true to experience and true to everyday living, whether in Outer Mongolia, icy Antarctica, the dunes of the Sahara, the peaks of the Andes or in the rain forests of Brazil. And above all, true to all those as yet unborn, a vast market that most tend to forget but will be yours because your text will discuss the purpose and meaning of life, not only as it is led but, more importantly, how it could be led for the betterment and enjoyment of everyone alive. How many beings really know why they've been born, or what their purpose is on Earth? And as for any notion of a life after death of the physical body, there is so much confusion, contradiction and ignorance, that the state of today's world is little better than that of cavemen; in both mentality and level of being there remains so much to be done. Could there be a greater challenge for any writer worth his salt than this? These are the issues you must address

and they include the themes of identity, purpose, values and the pursuit of real lasting happiness.

Remind your readers what many tend to overlook or even, perhaps, deny. Tell them that life on earth incorporates suffering, it's woven into the fabric of everyday living. It has infinite names: failure, disappointment, deception, regrets, frustration and so on. Each causes pain; it circumscribes human existence. Show me the man, woman, or child fortunate enough to know how to avoid the inevitable shocks of everyday living. You can't, for there's no escape. Who among you has not experienced frustrations, dissatisfactions, conflicts, anger, tears and brutal deception? Who can escape the immaturity and errors of judgement made in youth or the infirmities of age and the finality of death? No one, for these are the truths that are as far from fiction as Eden is from Hades. Your major task is to present, by means of fiction, the reality of the human condition, but in such a manner that your written narrative sustains the reader's interest throughout. And that, my friend, is no easy task; you need to both challenge and entertain your readers from page one. We have every confidence in you; just allow your fertile imagination to create the lies of fiction that tell the truth. And the truth in life, as in literature, is this: reality can't be proven; it can only be experienced. And so, in your writing, aim to bring your readers to new experiences, new ways of looking at things, especially at the things they see and feel every day, to new vistas and awareness of what is really out there but also what is deep inside them, their memories of past lives, their knowing of a collective consciousness, their hidden sense that we are all one, for our source is one.'

At this point, Nabi paused; he wanted the full weight of what he had said was required for modern fiction to succeed, to sink into my mind and heart. It was a lot to digest and would need *careful reflection later on for I had no doubts that he knew what he was talking about.*

He then concluded, Now, isn't that a real challenge? And so I leave you with this' – he then gave me a slip of paper – 'which is worth your full consideration and which I know will be of great use to you.'

What was written on that slip of paper is what I've appended to all my journals and is really the seed idea of all my serious writing done in my so-called retirement. And I'm talking of not so long ago…

"Wow!" Casey said to himself, as he read of this discovery. "I now know the source of that little paragraph that Noah had stuck so conspicuously inside every notepad. Its source is other-worldly, supernatural, where divinities, ascended masters and the hierarchy of angels live and have their 'magical' being. The contents of that tiny slip richly deserve to be the opening paragraph for it serves as the 'seed-idea' of all that follows. And what follows is, indeed, a text intended to appeal not only to everyone alive but – and this is its defining characteristic – also to all those 'yet to be born'. And it can do that because of its universal theme; Noah's journals are an open and frank discussion of the inescapable truths of the human condition and that hasn't changed for countless millennia; Gilgamesh, Buddha, Shri Krishna, Moses, Julius Caesar, Christ, Alfred the Great, Napoleon, Winston Churchill and Nelson Mandela are proof of that, but so am I and Sunita." And so are Noah's neighbours, even banter-loving, leg-pulling Hugh Dyfed Thomas and all of his drinking partners in this backwater of a township in mid-Wales, a place one local, who had just returned from holidays in rural Andalusia, called 'a one-horse funeral-parlour'.

Casey then saw that between the last entry and the next, Noah had put a cassette entitled 'My previous birth' (as told to me, word for word, by Nabi). The cassette was integral to the journals that were to become the novel that was to appeal to both the present and to all future generations of readers. Casey put the cassette into his PC and began to listen to what were Books Six and Seven, entitled 'Ruben's Story'.

Casey later discovered that the contents of the cassette had been copied into the journals and thus served as a back-up. It occurred to Casey that to make a back-up showed how important these pages were to Noah. Furthermore, although Casey had spoken to Noah by telephone, the conversations were brief and factual. Hearing the cassette at length, Casey was able to 'tune' into Nabi's voice that was clear, soothing and yet gently compelling. This is what he heard:

CHAPTER 10

'*Amy and Lee Dodge, a childless couple living in Wyoming, had spent a mini fortune on fertility drugs and treatments, all to no avail, and so, as a last resort, decided on adoption. Close to the state capital, Cheyenne, they found a well-run orphanage and made enquiries. After several visits and lengthy discussions with those who ran the orphanage, they happily applied for adoption papers. When all the standard enquiries and compulsory background checks had been made, the Dodge family became the proud parents of Ruben, who grew up with them not knowing anything about his early life, biological parents, mother-tongue or whether he had any siblings.*

'*One month after adoption, Amy and Lee were told "informally" by a former employee at the orphanage that Ruben had been "conceived in sin, abducted at birth and sold at five years of age to children traffickers in Brazil and that he had been 'salvaged' by a well-intentioned but impoverished Wyoming fireman who had paid for the child to be brought to his home, only then for the fireman to take the child to the orphanage in Cheyenne and leave him there!" The fireman had disappeared shortly thereafter and had not been seen since; he had left no contact number, no e-mail address and, according to the fire department, had resigned his post and left the service with full severance pay in his pocket. His decision to leave was his own and he did so amicably, thanking his colleagues and superiors for their "unfailing support and friendship". But he had given no reason for his resignation and none was sought.*

'She went on to say that all of this had happened in the last three months and had been reported in the local press. Cases of "missing persons" occur every day in the US and usually, without public interest or private money to support any search, interest in them soon runs cold and that was what happened with the fireman. He had vanished into the ether: speculation ran that aliens had abducted him! Furthermore, the orphanage was experiencing a severe shortage of funds and was therefore desperately seeking parents for adoption. In their eyes, Amy and Lee were ideal candidates and even suggested they take two children! The former employee concluded by saying that she had to stay anonymous because the name she went by in the orphanage was false as were her documents, and that's why she had to leave. She had looked after Ruben and really got to like him and so she applauded Amy and Lee's desire to foster him who, when he arrived, and this is Gospel-true, was very "sick, dehydrated and worryingly underweight; we all thought he was going to die".

'Everybody could see from his coffee-coloured skin colour, deep brown eyes and facial characteristics that he was not Amy and Lee's 'natural offspring' but had been adopted. His new parents were 'born-again Christians' and they loved him as much as they loved each other. After years of trying to start a family and spending hard-earned money on fertility drugs and treatments, they had now found 'Ruben'. He became their pride and joy and because both were very successful managers of hedge-funds and unusually lucky – or was it sheer skill? – at playing the stock market, had become incredibly rich and could offer little Ruben a king's upbringing. He went to the finest nursery, the best private school in Cheyenne, the state-capital

and progressed to Harvard where he studied *Artificial Intelligence Systems (AIS) and Robotics*. He proved to be immensely popular, not only because of his parents' wealth, but because of his innate qualities: unusually generous – some would say to the point of foolishness – he radiated self-confidence, possessed an enviable sense of humour, had very good looks and had no end of hobbies. He seemed to be interested in everything and not only with things to do with his studies of AI (Artificial Intelligence) and Robotics. His range of interests made him everyone's friend, simply because he could talk to each about their enthusiasms and mini-obsessions: whether it was animal magnetism, pop music, medical psychology, horse-racing, ancient astronaut theories, UFOs, Baroque architecture, medieval sexuality, classical art or modern poetry, he seemed able to contribute to the conversation. Everyone knew he was always reading something and that he had an almost photographic memory. And because examinations, at school, college and university, largely depend on "memorisation", he excelled. When asked about his successes at exams, he smiled and said it was a "matter of being pragmatic" and went on to say that the educational system he found himself in depended on "memory" and so he "developed his memory". It was as simple as that. Change the system and set other parameters and he would adapt to it. "Whether my approach shows intelligence or common-sense", he would tell his examiners, "I shall leave it to you all to discuss!"'

And then Casey saw that there was a post-script that read as follows:

'PS: When the world seemed to be his oyster, Ruben decided to *leave everything behind him and travelled to Europe "in search of himself". From the very occasional post-card sent to his doting but very anxious "parents", it seems he visited holy shrines in Greece, Spain, France and Italy before going to Egypt and finally to northern India. His last communication was from an ashram in Rishikesh, a famous hill-station in the foothills of the Himalayas. In short, in his previous life, Noah had gone from untold riches, honour and esteem to take the vows of poverty and obedience as a humble monk following a simple and very ancient path that led, ultimately, to "enlightenment", the goal and final reality of human existence. And so, according to Nabi, it was in this typical Indian ashram where Noah as Ruben, moved on to the next embodiment, the one which we as neutral readers, are now following.'*

For Casey, after having heard the tape twice through without any interruption, believed he could see why Noah seemed to be 'different' or 'eccentric', (a misfit was certainly not the right word) for he was always in touch with that greater reality that sacred writings and teachings always speak of and point towards. And so it was no great surprise that in the life just led, Noah had been 'chosen' to reawaken in himself and in others those great ancient truths that have always been there to be rediscovered by genuine and sincere seekers. As 'Ruben', Noah had shown extraordinary detachment; everything most of us want and strive for and even late in life, don't have, he had since adoption and enjoyed them for what they were. Not only had he doting parents, the best of home-life, education and friendships, he was also good-looking, very talented and popular, and enjoyed other people's company, especially those who shared his wave-length. And then, to turn his back on all of it, without a whimper or one single regret, is truly remarkable. And that left Casey wondering: how was Noah, when Ruben, able to say '*adios*' to it all and do so without second thoughts or regrets? The answer, Casey muses, must be straightforward; he undoubtedly had a glimpse of a higher vision or a higher calling that showed him real values, true treasures, a vision that held deep significance and meaning throughout all of human existence. He clearly had come to see the futility of most of human actions and activities, the hollowness of what we find in ordinary, everyday life and that what he once used to worry about were 'neither here nor there'. And so, logically, he looked elsewhere, seeking something, let's call it, the 'good and true' that not only existed but could communicate itself to him, the discovery – and acquisition of which – would lead him to eternal joy and happiness in this life, in this incarnation. It was that search in his previous life that had led him in this life, eventually, to Nabi who, allegedly, knew everybody's previous lives, especially his own.

Casey was finding these entries fascinating; the details relating to Noah's 'former life on earth', the role of the mysterious fireman without whom, who can say what would have befallen Ruben? And Ruben's dramatic volte-face that made him turn his back on the very successful life he led in the US, only for him to end his days in far-away India, in an ashram where he lived the simple life following the rules and relations of 'monastic life' as a humble monk!

Casey wondered if Noah had wanted to know of his other embodiments and if he ever asked Nabi. But nothing that followed in the journals mentioned such a wish. Casey was also curious as to how Noah's story would continue; in brief, how would Noah follow on after such an extraordinary event that revealed actual and detailed knowledge of his previous embodiment. From Casey's own studies, he gladly accepted the principle of reincarnation – an eternal repetition or cycle until enlightenment – and would have loved to learn about some of his own previous lives, too!

In Book Seven of the journals and after the entry above, there was a gap in the writing that lasted over nine months. The next entry read:

I have decided to write the remainder of my journal as a novel and thus complete what Nabi asked me to do. How else am I to put to good use my time spent in the Mystery schools – and what I learned in them – if not in my writings? For I have seen and heard things very few mortals have heard or seen, things that all thinking human beings would love to know about, albeit second-hand. And I have not forgotten that my audience is to include those yet awaiting rebirth, that endless ocean of souls that will seek, eventually, enlightenment and release from the eternal cycle of birth–death–rebirth. I know this because I was taken to a celestial plane where souls were awaiting incarnation; in a vast enclosure called the 'Hall of Waiting', I saw 'souls at rest' under the protection of the angels of destiny, planetary beings who not only rule the happenings of physical life but are also the builders of the soul-world. I then realised that the existence of such souls awaiting rebirth explain what we on Earth call human love. We think we fall in love, produce children, live our lives and then meet our creator! No! That view is totally upside down! A soul waiting to be born is the trigger that sets off the love-stories that are so central to human life and activity and fill the pages of countless novels in every language!

Casey, when he read these lines, realised he was at the true beginning of the novel that Noah was determined to complete during his retirement and in his 'autumn of life'. Although what he had read and had been able to digest so far had gripped his attention from page one, he was now on the verge of discovering even greater 'truths' or 'realities', if that were at all possible. Detailed information about Noah's previous embodiment as Reuben had exceeded all his expectations but now to be told of a 'visit' to the Hall of Waiting that has its location on a celestial site or plane called the soul-world and is where millions of souls 'rest' before their next embodiment, a desire on their part that explains the mysterious phenomenon of human love on Earth, was mind-blowing and yet, somehow conceivable, plausible even. If true, all of us on Planet Earth see things 'upside-down' and so the question follows; what else do we view as upside-down?

Casey suddenly felt nervous; what other things that we commonly take for granted would be shown to be untrue, unhelpful or even downright mad? And so, Casey turned to Book Eight which indeed deals with a statement made by Nabi and which is underlined in his journal and written in that unmistakable calligraphic script used by Noah to emphasise his message. So, let us all now return to Noah's entry that begins a new stage and a turning-point in the novel's structure and content:

Nabi's remark that at birth, the pattern of the skies holds the blueprint for the life to be led, gave me food for thought. For Nabi never said anything untrue or unhelpful; he always spoke words of wisdom and this particular statement explained in a nutshell what the future held for every soul born. As an ascended master, he knew decades before it happened that I would re-fashion my diaries into a novel that was intended to appeal to the widest possible audience. Translation into world languages would inevitably follow for everyone deserves the opportunity to know the reason for their birth and how best to lead life on Planet Earth. The world around me was in a real mess; wars, civil strife, hunger, disease, corruption, injustices – the list grows daily – and so anything that could end such madness had to be supported. I had been given the means to show my fellow-men how to live in harmony and in peace, both necessary to lead a meaningful existence. For me, Nabi held the keys to the kingdom of Heaven and had given me those very keys to lead mankind from their 'living Hell' to the gates of the Promised Land and open them forever. It was an undertaking suffering humanity would praise, applaud and encourage but exceptionally few would ever agree to do. Hadn't Sunita already told me that no more than five people on the planet had been found to 'assist' me in my mission, but not yet? I was alone on the battle-field, but I would not be alone in the thick of battle. That said, I knew the time had come: I was ready. I had been specially trained for such an overwhelming mission and had at my side not only Nabi but a whole host of celestial beings willing me on. There was no turning back; heaven could no longer wait! Besides, I was no longer a youth but already advanced in age, an old fogey to teenagers, an old fart to middle-aged well-wishers and undoubtedly both a fart and an eccentric to most of my contemporaries. But so what?

How many men, when subject to conflicting emotions, see the better course of action but, sadly, pursue the worse? For it is generally accepted that human error has its source in our giving assent to things not clearly perceived, as if we were working in the penumbra, cast by doubt or uncertainty. But that was not my situation. Time was passing more and more quickly – the quicker as you age – and no other task was more urgent. Follow me now and see how, in my 'late' retirement, I began my mission in earnest. The outcome is seen better, not with what I made of life, but rather what life has made of me. Readers now know that I had been 'chosen' to pioneer a new way of living; indeed, I soon came to see my mission as an 'experiment in the art of living' that had its source in ethereal planes well above the norm but yet was so designed to be led by human beings on Planet Earth. But we on Earth had lost our way, had lost contact with our divine source, and so were no different to lost sheep aimlessly roaming bleak moorland looking for the shepherd and verdant pastures. Profoundly aware of this, I had willingly decided to carry the banner first given to Sunita, my one-time wife and best friend who now was constantly active in the star-world. And to perform such a noble deed, I had been sent to sacred Mystery schools at undisclosed locations but always 'accessible', so I was reliably informed, to souls who genuinely seek a higher calling. I had such a calling and, if we are to believe Nabi, and I do unreservedly, even before birth I had always yearned for such a calling; it was part of me, just as my face, arms and legs are part of me. But the physical trigger to make that calling a reality had been the devastating shock of Sunita's 'moving on'; an event that compelled me to take stock and re-evaluate all my values and priorities.

Yet, even before her death from eclampsia, I had always been aware of what I prefer to call 'other-worldly things'. I brought into this life – by virtue of my previous embodiment –an awareness and a corpus of experience that had shown me the emptiness of almost everything that happens in everyday life, whether in our work, our conversations or in our so-called leisure activities, I took it upon myself to see whether there existed something that was truly meaningful and worthwhile and that, if at all possible, led to a lasting happiness. In short, I longed to discover whether there was something that not only made sense of this life, but would, in the next and throughout all of eternity, guarantee me supreme joy and bliss. Long before I became a conscientious teacher of math, I had sensed that modern life didn't offer what I believed it should offer and what was that. If not the time to pursue and promote culture and cultural interests? Sadly, too, I had found it increasingly difficult to accept the fact that modern education no longer offered what I maintained it should always offer. And that, in a nutshell, was the opportunity for all pupils to discover and develop innate talents. For each of us has talents, somewhere, very often hidden and often only discovered by virtue of a life-or-death situation, an accident perhaps, or what seems to be an inexplicably bizarre encounter or event. I became more and more disillusioned with educational policies that were not pupil-centred but result-driven; it was the beginning of an intellectual crisis that led me to believe that most human beings were nothing other than a 'species of the dead', a rare species at that. The outcome of this crisis was for me to turn more and more to my diaries; it was in these where I felt compelled to enter my thoughts and queries and do so with ever greater urgency. In so doing, I became, unknowingly at first, my own critic and commentator for I had realised that the vast majority of those around me were not yet 'ready' to listen to my ideas. To change such a mind-set, especially with regard to secondary school educational policy and to inner personal development, I had to resort to what I called 'claps of thunder and heavenly fireworks', needed, so I believed, to awaken the dormant minds and senses of the masses. As a result, don't be surprised to find in my diaries what to many may seem to be outrageous, even absurd ideas!

I didn't set out to be confrontational or take on the mantle of a rebel, but if those in authority refused to listen to my well-founded suggestions and concerns, so be it, I am at liberty to fix them in ink for others to read after my passing and carry the battle forwards! I knew I was walking on a tightrope, living totally on the edge, seeking answers to questions few, if any, had the knowledge or the courage to ask. As a direct consequence of my struggles and disagreements with various educational initiatives, I came to prefer, even long before retirement, the company of characters in literature. But not only in literature; I also found congenial company in figures (many well-known) in paintings and sculptures. For me, they were more 'alive', vibrantly more alive, than many of the automatons walking our streets. The sleepwalkers I commonly met in cafes, supermarkets, large stores, public transport and restaurants were fictions fitted out in a coat of flesh. Real-life people inhabit novels, plays and paintings, and wear paper-thin garments made from natural wood fibre or longer-lasting clothes made from canvas, oils or pure marble.

A private conversation with Hamlet, Falstaff, or Mr Pickwick or a silent meditation with the various portraits of Handel, Oscar Wilde or Nietzsche meant more to me than the frothy chatter about popular TV programmes, current cinema or sports stars, immoral politicians or about the shenanigans and lifestyles of the mega-rich. But don't stop there. Major figures in ancient history – Babylonian, Persian, Greek or Roman – seemed to offer me much more than the robots and automatons that roam the streets of any large city today. And so when in London (not often enough for me), I would always visit the Portrait Gallery near Trafalgar Square. Once inside, surrounded by the portraits of eminent men and women, many of whom had striven to leave the world a 'better place' than when they entered it, I was in my element and would happily spend time in enjoyable contemplation of universally admired works of art. After all, 'real works of art', in literature, sculpture, architecture and in engineering, to name a few, 'speak' to us, as we often say, and so I used to speak back to them. I haven't yet met another soul who admits to doing the same, but I doubt if I am totally alone. And if I am, so be it; I don't see it as a problem and that's why I'm proudly unafraid to say so. When I speak to Nabi, a real, authentic celestial being who is 'at home' in the infinite star-world, our conversations are 'alive', full of real interest and always relevant to the matter in hand. We share the same radar, as did Sunita, and others, whom I met in the ancient Mystery schools where the wisdom of the ages is preserved and passed on. In my first 'lesson', I was told – and let this be my first 'revelation' to readers of this novel – that Jesus Christ attended such schools. After all, the last mention of the word teacher in the gospels is when aged twelve. Thereafter, so it seems, he 'vanished' from sight only to return when aged thirty, a man with a mission. Clearly, in those deliberately 'undocumented' eighteen years of existence, he was being prepared for his life's work. And that, in sum, was nothing less than the salvation of humanity. He showed us how to live dignified and socially useful lives extolling the virtues of peace, harmony and unity, all of which depend on unconditional love. All great teachers of mankind concern themselves with how we, as human beings, live our everyday lives and how we behave towards each other; they question our attitudes, intentions and motives while lifting our sights to higher, more noble levels of co-existence. And whatever advice, counsel or guideline given, has been given so that we all can live 'more abundantly' and thus fulfil our human potential. No doubt, for some, perhaps for many, 'more abundantly' would better translate as fatter wage-packets, bigger profits and ever increasing port-folios!

To my mind, even when quite young, there was a world of difference between the verbs to 'live' and to 'exist'; animals, plants, trees and stones exist but only creative human beings 'live'. It was a distinction that I had made to myself long before my 'special training' in the Mystery schools. And once inside such schools, that distinction became much more profound; not a day passed without a teacher reminding us of our mission to 'wake others up'. In short, I had begun to see little or no difference between the daily lives 'lived out' by countless millions and the simple 'existence' of animals, farm or otherwise, plants or minerals. From direct observation, I even believed that on a few occasions, I had correctly identified humans who, because of their behaviour and social habits, 'had just emerged from the animal kingdom!'

As a self-declared freethinker, I gave no credence to the account in Genesis of the creation of the world in 'six days' and saw no possible reason why the Supreme Creator would need to rest on the 'seventh'! Such views as these I discreetly confined to my diaries; my deep interest in oriental teachings ensured that I had no wish to hurt the feelings of others and certainly not face-to-face! That said, if I discovered that I had inadvertently upset someone's feelings, I felt genuine remorse. For that is the type of person I aimed to be but in my 'private writings', my precious diaries, I said what I honestly thought and believed. In public, always modest and courteous and ever-conscious of the feelings of others, each of whom I regarded as my 'next-of-kin', but in my writings, I far preferred to shoot from the hip!

How else was a sleep-walking, self-indulgent, trivial-

pursuits-seeking humanity to be awakened? And that very question lay at the heart of the mission entrusted to me by Nabi. If we see the mass of humanity as an inert force, an image often used by my spiritual teachers in the sacred Mystery schools, what are those 'awake' to do in order to resurrect such a dead mass? How are the very few 'fully awake souls' to guide those 'half-awake beings', the sleepwalkers, the dormant majority to realise their full human potential? If somnambulism is part and parcel of everyday existence because it's built into the very fabric of the human condition, how can mankind be made aware of the fact and shown how to transcend it. For in transcendence lay a greater reality, the reality of our vast potential that all too often lay untapped because unknown. That very question was posed to me every single day of my so-called 'sabbatical leave' that the state had so generously given me to recover from my recent loss. And every day, my response to that question underwent a subtle change; there was no easy quick-fix answer. An inert sleeping humanity is similar to a dead-weight, unmovable object; similar but not the same and so when, as teachers of physics will tell us, that object meets an irresistible force, something is bound to happen.

A change occurs that has the effect of animating or lifting that immense mass. And that force, for me, was none other than Nabi. In his precepts and guidelines for human conduct on Planet Earth was found the manna from Heaven that perfectly met and nourished the needs of the human spirit; and it was the same nourishment I was offered in my conversations with, inter alia, **Hamlet, Prospero, Mr Pickwick,** *the* **Little Prince** *and with* **Alice in Wonderland.** *If I could somehow recreate that self-same manna in my writing, I would certainly be able to connect with all my readers, now and in the future, too. And so, in order to reach out* *to my 'next-of-kin', narrative techniques – the ways and means of all wordsmiths – had to be devised and put to their best use. Above all, I had to connect with all my readers' interests. If possible, I had to invent and exploit the use of 'literary fireworks', verbal thunderclaps, narrative sheets of lightning that clothed seemingly outrageous themes and happenings, no matter how preposterous, that can and do happen to certain individuals. If you don't believe me, listen to the news, read your national newspapers, visit your nearest A&E unit, read epitaphs on gravestones, look at factual TV documentaries that probe the weird and wonderful that include ancient astronaut theories, the paranormal, mysterious land structures, UFOs and so on.*

In brief, incredible things happen and often happen to the next-door neighbour, a Joey Jones or a Shirley Shortbread. Such events I also had to describe but in a manner that didn't, in any way, frighten or deter potential readers but rather would seduce all of them, willy-nilly. All readers need to be entertained and their interest sustained from paragraph one; I planned to achieve this while simultaneously dropping petals of wisdom for them to eat and drink as if 'real' magic mushrooms, the true and everlasting bread of heaven. I would attempt to become a literary chameleon, even speak with several 'forked-tongues', for the best of writing is always imbued with several layers of meaning and interpretation.

As such, it cannot fail to appeal to all levels of society, especially to the biased views of the so-called 'man-in-the-street, the non-discerning 'Lumpenproletariat', as the Germans colourfully describe such a class of society.

I firmly believe my eminent teachers in the Schools of Mystery taught me how to write such narrative fireworks and do so without burning one single human hair. They told me that this is what third millennial readers hungered for; they longed to read texts that addressed them as they were but could lead them to where their heart of hearts told them they could go and feel at home, just as much as Nabi felt at home in the infinite space of the 'star-world'. They yearned for novels that released the 'soul' within, their soul that they felt lay trapped and imprisoned in a coat of flesh; third millennial novels, claimed Nabi, had to allow all such imprisoned souls to walk in the snow and leave no trace behind; write love-letters in the sand that no tide could ever erase; point to stars in the firmament that could be touched, caressed and kissed and if so desired, be taken home in one's pocket! I knew such a literary objective seemed beyond my ken, beyond my level of ability – some would say the aim was virtually impossible – and they had a point, but I had other-worldly help.

For everyone, consciously or not, is searching for his own 'true identity' and for a meaning or purpose. We all do so while facing the same life-issues; growing up, going to school, taking exams, finding a suitable job and partner as well as suffering the inevitable setbacks, disappointments and pains of everyday living. Add to these the inescapable process of growing old, the infirmities it brings leading to decay and death. Aware of these built-in realities, we all naturally seek a way-out to avoid pain, suffering, adversity and the 'thousand natural shocks that flesh is heir to'. If life on Earth incorporates suffering, what can be done to alleviate it, if not stop it? Is there a method, or a teaching or a manual that can show us how to escape what is built in to existence? And that urgent question leads me to my second revelation; all pupils in the Mystery schools, so I was told, are given this task, and I myself had to face it: Find a better guideline or teaching for living than these few words of Christ; 'Love your neighbour as yourself'.

I will not reveal here the outcome of the exercise in the Mystery school but when given it, I knew it would be something I could take back with me to my urban sixth form college in Lancashire. I waited several years – and I can't reasonably explain the delay – but years passed before I was guided by something inside me to pose that same question to all sixteen-year-olds-plus in the college. I discussed it with the principal and with the head of religious studies and both immediately agreed that the question should be put, not to every sixth form college but to every school in the land and that is what eventually took place. Interest in the competition became so intense that I kept a diary of what took place and that 'report' now follows.

CHAPTER 11

In order to celebrate the life of Mother Teresa of Calcutta, this at least was the public reason to launch the idea, the principal created a template that every school and college anywhere could use. The aim was to establish an open competition in which all pupils were invited to participate. Pupils and students were asked to write in one sentence something that would be of use to everybody, not only in the school or college but to everybody everywhere; the model given was 'Love your neighbour as yourself'. A prize donated by local businessmen was to be awarded to the winning entrant. Given the serious nature of the competition, it was agreed that an additional five prizes would be given to competitors ranked second to sixth. All prize-winning sentences, maxims or statements would be published in local, regional – and if good fortune smiled at us –also in national newspapers as well as be sent viral to all educational establishments throughout the UK! All entries had to be submitted within one calendar month! I was both excited and curious before it dawned on me that no one had been chosen to adjudicate. I approached the principal voicing that very question. After all, the prize-winning entry would become national, if not global property, within twenty-four hours. Educational prizes, whether in school or college or even at university are, in general, very modest, but to come up with a sentence that could match – surpass was out of the question! – the magnificent teaching of a world teacher such as Jesus Christ, what sort of prize could we offer? No surprise then that in no time at all the whole college wanted to know what the prize would be. As one astute student in the Lower Sixth said, 'The mental energy and time needed to come up with a statement that would cater for everybody alive as well as those yet to be born had to be worth millions!' And when the other students learned of his 'claim', they all agreed and demanded that the prize be known before any submission was to be made. Clearly, the college authorities, the education department, parents and parent organisations realised that to talk of millions was a 'no-brainer'. Which state college or school could afford such an amount?

The head of religious studies was the hour-glassed shaped Miss Kay Riqueza, a nubile thirty-three-year-old beauty from Murcia in Spain who thought that the prize should consist of a parcel of goodies, one of which was to be a fully paid two-week holiday in SE Spain for the student/pupil's entire family. The idea of a 'bundle of gifts' appealed to the majority of 'candidates' and so Miss Riqueza earned a shedload of bonus-points and would be seen walking along corridors, entering and leaving classrooms smiling from ear to ear. Her sun-kissed face was seen by one of my students who one day entered my class, saying, 'Sir, is anything wrong with Miss Riqueza? She walks around the college like a dog with two tails!'

The class roared out in laughter and clapped their hands and stamped their feet and gave each other 'high-fives'. But that was not the end of it because that same student, Jason Shard was his name, then began to complain about the competition saying that the task set was infinitely harder than any other school or college competition to date! More clapping and cheering and even louder 'high-fives' followed in quick succession. I learned later that razor-sharp Jason Shard took a delegation of likeminded students to the principal's office asking who was to judge the competition; all insisted 'it should not be Miss Riqueza 'cos she had her favourites in every class'. *Student-power finally compelled the principal to seek out a competent judge; after due research and inquiry, he found a Professor Marmaduke Mink, a graduate in theology from an unnamed university somewhere in the wastes of Nebraska in the USA, an Anglophile who had recently returned to his roots in a nearby university town where he was Head of Theological Studies. Marmaduke was chosen because nobody had heard of him and, as far as anyone knew, had never had anything published and so according to the principal, Marmaduke (Marmite to all the students and staff!) was the ideal choice.*

After all, he knew no one in any school or college in Chorley and thus would be totally unbiased. Moreover, his certifiable qualifications in 'religious matters' gave him the credentials needed to judge such a unique competition. When photos that were no different to mugshots of Marmaduke were circulated on Facebook and shown in various local, national and transnational newspapers, there was a gasp because Marmaduke was an unholy mix of Al Capone, Popeye's Olive and King Kong's first cousin! This is not the time or place to mention the countless comments made by journalists, newspaper readers, parents and many of the students (not forgetting those of pupils' nation-wide) who were also fans of Facebook but suffice to say that very few were positive, polite or even printable! An entire chapter could easily be devoted to the comments made by such individuals but that would distract the reader from the import of the competition. Besides, it would be totally unchristian to publish such remarks, no matter how 'inventive' or screamingly funny, because it would not be in keeping with the noble and humane purpose of the challenge. For his labours, Marmaduke was to receive three copies, written in Gothic script using gold-leaf paint and beautifully bound with a silken tassel, of all six winning entries. The art teacher, the colourful and well-liked Mr Moses Morrison, from Edinburgh in Scotland, whose passion was Classical Indian Temple Music, was appointed to produce the three copies for the self-effacing Marmaduke, the adjudicator supreme. When news of the unique competition was made public in the local rag, almost every college and school in the country and beyond wanted to mount the same competition! Good news, because relatively rare travels even faster than bad news and so what immediately had begun as a local affair had overnight come of both national and international, indeed global; such is the power of today's internet and world-wide-web!

In the UK, at least, the principal was delighted to hear of such unintended universal interest and immediately agreed to their requests of using the theme of his competition in their institution. What had innocently begun as a college challenge suddenly had grown wings, one hundred times more powerful than Pegasus, and had entered the world's vast educational arena; nations especially interested were: Brazil, Japan, India, Spain, Germany, Nigeria, the USA, Sri Lanka and Israel. Now listen to the prizes offered by certain individuals abroad; a philanthropic Texan banker offered a private jet as first prize together with a six figure sum of American dollars! Two Chinese billionaires offered the winner a penthouse in Beijing's most fashionable Sanlitun district, the city's richest and equivalent to London's Mayfair, but no money. Given that tipping in mainland China is forbidden, the absence of a monetary prize was in keeping with that nation's noble ancestry and thus to those few who knew of Chinese customs, no real surprise! The vast majority of entrants, however, who wished to participate in this unique world-wide competition, were saddened at the lack of a cash prize.

A family in India offered a mini-palace on the Ganges, a villa in Tuscany and three royal elephants! A Brazilian billionaire offered one of his four virgin daughters (the winner could choose which!) and a dowry of two million English pounds; an unnamed Japanese politician and owner of a hugely successful software company offered the winning entrant three years paid study of Theology and Philosophy at a prestigious university in the UK, followed by a fully-paid guided tour of all the world's sacred sites. In addition, a pension beginning at twenty-one for life; the amount, undoubtedly generous, was not disclosed because immediately after his tempting offer, he was impeached for tax evasion. Other institutions offered a host of different prizes, every one of which was published in national papers and advertised on TV networks.

When the candidates heard of such mouth-watering prizes, they asked the organisers to make the competition international with an international panel of judges. They wanted to be able to share in the global interest and have access to all the mind-blowing prizes on offer. Although unconfirmed, it was widely rumoured that Jason Shard suggested to dishy Miss Riqueza that the college should hold a competition to discover what students thought of the prizes on offer and what, indeed, they believed was the best. It was a great suggestion and so she put that very question to all of her students in each of her classes; a ballot box was placed on her desk and the vote taken. All the boys chose the Brazilian billionaire, a Mr Camelot Iguacu's offer, of one of his virgin daughters plus the £2m dowry. It was said that the girls', with very few exceptions, chose the offer made by the now sadly *impeached Japanese politician.*

With such global interest, mass-media frenzy and unbelievable prizes on offer, the principal soon felt totally out of his depth and so called an emergency staff meeting. He simply admitted his 'incompetence' and piously asked his staff to help him choose the next step: 'What would be the best thing to do for the college?' They sympathised deeply with his quandary, confessing they, too, had no real answer. In the face of such an impasse, cone-shaped Miss Drum, the music teacher, politely suggested that the college contact the Chief Education Officer (C.E.O.) and seek his advice. And that's what happened but then the CEO, aware of the prestige to be gained by the global interest in the competition, contacted his MP, a cabinet minister, who in turn, but off the record, it must be said, asked the prime minister for his advice. A cabinet meeting was summoned the very next day! A solution had to be found quickly, they were told, there was no other option. In the meanwhile, hordes of paparazzi, TV crews, secret government agents, conspiracy theorists and, in particular, anti-religionists descended on the college wanting to interview both the staff and would-be candidates. Amid the delirium and wild excitement that raged both in-and-outside the college gates, parents of students in every class, mine included, went to the Citizen's Advice Bureau seeking urgent guidance. Most of them wanted to win a prize, some even more so than their offspring, but sagely did not say as much; all of them complained that their 'darling son or daughter', because of the frenzy in and outside the school buildings, had no real space or time to think of a suitable answer and so their chances of winning the competition were 'being jeopardised'.

The C.A.B members agreed wholeheartedly because they, too, had sons and daughters at the college (or if not, knew someone who did) and, naturally, also wanted to have a slice of the fabulously rich cake on offer. Who in their right mind wouldn't do everything possible to have a chance of winning such magnificent prizes! I was well aware of such complaints and in fact agreed with the parents. In the Mystery schools, 'pupils' do have time and space to think but, even despite optimum conditions, we all found it exceedingly difficult to match the statement. That much I can reveal here and now but it can't be too much of a surprise. Despite that, the armies of reporters, TV crews, 'secret' government agents, the curious and especially out-and-out atheists were all hoping that an untutored and uncluttered young mind would find a statement that could surpass the fundamental tenet of Christianity. What a world scoop that would be! Logic militated strongly against such a statement being found but the lure of 'what if?' drew everybody into its web; major bookmakers, Ladbrokes, William Hill, Coral, Paddy Power, Betfred and a host of others worldwide offered tempting odds to win-seeking punters. The whole planet, so it seemed, was caught up in what had begun as a local college competition. Behind it all, I strongly suspected that Nabi was somehow involved, but as always, was keeping his playing-cards close to his chest. The 'competition' clearly had a greater but, as yet, unseen purpose.

To return to my own efforts when in the Mystery schools, I remember a tutor who always wore a purple sari and had been an 'orientalist' in one of her incarnations. She made a point of mentioning a sentence that she had learnt by heart when very young: the Self lives in the hearts of all and everything.

She always found a moment to recite it during her lectures and, occasionally, would write it very slowly on the blackboard in beautiful calligraphic handwriting and would leave it there for days on end. When I was first introduced to such a concept, I immediately saw its relevance and value; it was a truly inspirational statement, given to help us focus on what was required to solve the riddle. I liked it because it lacked the compulsion of the 'Love your neighbour...' teaching that set the standard. That said, I was then told that this 'truth' was written on every single fig tree found in the gardens of each of the Mystery schools: one fig tree to each school. With surprise overlain by curiosity, I took a walk in the 'groves' as they were called and, sure enough, at the base of the only fig tree found in the groves I saw the statement that had been lovingly 'engraved' deeply into the bark. And then I noticed beneath the sentence a small chest which I opened and saw that it held a book, the size and thickness of the average Y/A novel. I randomly opened a page of the book and saw a list of names of former students – so I was told later – who had attended the Mystery schools; name, date and nationality, beautifully written, were clearly legible. And as I read some names that jumped out at me, the book, suddenly and of its own accord, went to the page that held the very last entry. I waited and waited until I realised I had been invited to enter my details, too. And so without further ado, I proudly added my details in my best handwriting. I say 'best handwriting' but I believe, no, not believe, I know for certain, that my hand was being guided; my details, Noah Azrael Salmon, together with that day's date and my 'current' nationality, were written in handwriting I could never imitate. I certainly held the pen but I swear before Heaven it was not Noah Salmon who did the writing. My entry surpassed the writing found in those wonderful medieval Bibles that pious, selfless monks illustrated year upon year and that became their life's work. But that was not all. Read on, dear reader, Read on.

As soon as I (or the invisible hand) had entered my details, the book closed itself and then re-opened at page one! And what I saw will appear to most, if not to all, readers of this unusual tale as utter balderdash, total nonsense, even as impossible! But no. Such interpretations or reactions would be wrong. Trust me on this!

The very first name entered was that of Nabi, the nationality given was 'Venusian' and the date recorded was 88,000, BC! In short, Nabi was some 90,000 years old! I was astonished, amazed, momentarily not knowing what to think or believe. But then, what does the notion of immortality convey to us? What does eternity, or forever and forever, really consist of, or mean? For, undoubtedly, where Sunita and Nabi now 'lived', time as we know it, has no relevance or meaning whatsoever! What does the figure one million years mean to Jupiter or Mercury or to a grain of sand, an asteroid or to a sperm-whale? Nothing! But on earth, we humans are time-bound; we grow up watching the clock, forever asking the time, waiting for the next birthday, anniversary, bank holiday, the next film, game or meal. Rolex watches can cost an arm and a leg; church bells can weigh a ton and be heard for miles and miles; every school, institute, shop, office, prison, hospital, factory, sports venue has a current time-table.

So then, how on earth had this 'book' been able to endure such a length of time without any sign of corruption, not a single smudge of wear and tear, not one single ink-blot? How many climate changes had it endured? How many floods, snow-falls, dust-storms, twisters, forest-fires, Covid-19-type viruses and pollutants had it survived? Every reader would ask the self-same questions, right? But then what came to mind – and I can't explain why – the gift Sunita gave to me (a lotus flower) for use on my journey and mission was, I had been instructed, indestructible. And Nabi confirmed its other qualities, too. So, I had to assume, that this 'Book of Destiny' as I came to call it, possessed the very same attributes. There was no other rational, bona fide explanation.

Now, although the book dated from aeons ago, the number of names did not reach one hundred; I remember very clearly that I was number 95...

At this point, Nabi has told me to tell you all that, as a further 'gift', and only by virtue of divine dispensation, I can reveal to my curious readers some names that I clearly remember seeing in the Book of Destiny: Moses, Buddha, Shri Krishna, Socrates, Mohammad, Leonardo da Vinci, Shakespeare, Tesla and Alexander von Humboldt; *five other names are in my head but because I am not totally certain, I prefer not to include them but any reader curious enough to want to know the 'forgotten five' should contact the publishers who will willingly provide the five names – all of whom are famous figures. But that was not the end of my discovery of the fig tree and its chest of treasures.*

I soon learnt that every student is invited to plant a tree of their choice in the sacred grove; any tree could be chosen because in ancient Mystery schools, the soil is fed by an elixir that guarantees 'immortality' after full growth is attained. I chose the bo tree, sometimes called the 'peepul' or 'pipal' tree, and have been told that it's thriving and has become a favourite meditation site for Nabi. Through an intergalactic grape-vine, I have also been told that Socrates and da Vinci like to meditate there on full moon as does that purple sari-wearing tutor of mine in the Mystery school. I was further informed that she was also one of the 'star-people' and had been one of the very best 'disciples' of Nabi aeons ago. I recall vividly one day, just after she had written her favourite statement on the blackboard, that she thought this favourite sentence of hers came very close to meeting the conditions of the competition. She didn't believe that it was more powerful or more convincing than the words of Christ, yet could be of service and of immediate help to humanity. Readers should know that the statement, 'Whatever lives is full of the Lord' is a well-known concept in ancient Indian teachings written in Sanskrit but that she had added the words 'all and everything' to it. She thereby wanted to show us that whatever lives had to include animals, plants and minerals because they also are creations from the hand of the Supreme Creator and if you believe in such a Being, she was absolutely right. 'All and everything' means what it says, for creation consists of unity and totality. Our world is of necessity filled with things, particular objects, but they each exist within a single order. Nothing or nobody is excluded.

CHAPTER 12

Having been reminded to write in my diaries details of my experiences in the Mystery schools so that readers could draw real benefit from my stay there, I saw the competition as a very useful device to do just that. And that is why I threw myself heart and soul into it; I also knew it was a wish close to Nabi's heart.

It should now be mentioned that in my maths class in Chorley, there was an outstanding female pupil who was everybody's best friend. Her name was Lisa and it was known that she had spent several late-nights alone in her girl-cave and had really given her heart and soul to the task, but despite her superhuman efforts and best of intentions believed that the statement she had finally chosen would fail. She was everybody's favourite because she was so good-natured and wanted the best for everybody and had a special love for animals and plants. At weekends and during school holidays – and later when at college, too – she would help at the local vet's and worked for free. She had a gift for mathematics and music, but her passion was astrology; so much so she told her best friends that she was not an 'earth-person' – in fact, according to her, no one was! – and felt in tune with the night sky, its constellations and with the moon. That said, she 'asked her space brothers and sisters' for guidance and when it came, she wrote whatever was given to her on her entry form with the utmost care and precision and then signed the form and placed it neatly in an extra-securely sealed envelope. On the last day of the month, she happily carried her envelope, in person, to the red-coloured submissions box outside the principal's office. Once her envelope was securely placed inside the box, she inwardly smiled knowing that her submission would give the adjudicators food for thought. Her envelope was the last to be posted and lay on the very top of a huge pile of others; there were no limits to individual entries and, expectedly, everybody wanted to win, even if the college-prize was to be nothing more than a book voucher worth £50 only!

As she left the submissions-box that supposedly held the blood-and-sweat of scores of entries aimed at the prize, Lisa's mind turned to the competition's focus: the creation of a sentence, a message for humanity that was timeless in its essence. Was there anywhere on Planet Earth, hidden or 'lost' or buried in a library or bank-vault or in a former monastery or castle, now in ruins, or even under the sea, a message, a sentence that could equal the words of Jesus? She had read of the lost city of Atlantis, of El Dorado, of the destruction of priceless libraries whether in Alexandria, Jerusalem, in Rome or in Babylon, in ancient Greece and elsewhere; maybe somewhere in one of such books or documents or archives there was a sentence – perhaps even more than one! – that matched the matchless words of 'Love your neighbour…'

It was humanly possible, was it not, given that in every age there have been masters of wisdom? Buried deep under the sand-dunes of ancient lands in Arabia, or concealed in tombs no longer accessible to us today or inscribed on clay tablets ravaged by time or war, there probably was such a teaching, but who today is really interested in finding such? The reality is, we do have a teaching to help us all to live in peace and harmony which, if practised by all, would lead to 'heaven on earth', the kingdom of Utopia some have written about! Every sane, civilised, honest *person knows this even though theologians, imams, rabbis, priests, clerics, Biblical scholars argue endlessly about the 'persona' of Christ, about his miracles, the resurrection and the validity of the gospels. Not to mention those who deny his existence outright! None of their debates, discourses, conferences, assemblies, rituals, ceremonies, or traditions have ever led to a statement or to a teaching that is so simple to understand, so immediately accessible and so in tune with man's reason. Lisa was well aware of all this but she remained curious and open to the discovery of texts and documents that may be similar in nature. With the help of her 'hidden friends' in the skies, she may well have been introduced to such texts and documents.*

The deadline had passed but what, in the meanwhile, had happened off-stage, so to speak? Did the various governments come up with a policy to suit all parties? Yes, they did; it was agreed that the winning entrant, not of any particular school or college, but of each country, should go forward to an Olympic-style world competition to be held in...? And that was the next dilemma because the panel of adjudicators could not decide on a suitable venue; a venue had to be selected that was 'neutral' to all-comers A vote was taken and Beijing was chosen; China had not taken part in the competition and thus no Chinese candidate would be involved. It should be mentioned that Beijing won by one single vote; other venues mentioned were Easter Island, Lapland, Patagonia and Transylvania. All nations agreed to the Chinese capital as the venue and so it was that 144 candidates were flown to the former Olympic Village in Beijing in September, 2016 and the overall winner was to be announced on October 13 of that same year. So as not to bore readers or distract from the great interest such a competition must hold for humanity, suffice to say that Lisa's submission, The Supreme Being lives in the hearts of all, won her school's and nation's vote but she did not win the prize. A jealous and greedy sixteen-year-old student in the college waited until Lisa had 'posted' her entry and was well out of sight. This girl – let's call her Robyn Banks – somehow managed to lift it off the top of the pile, opened it, read the entry and then tore it up and re-wrote it on another piece of paper, sealed it in an envelope and dropped it into the box and then ran home. Lisa's entry was torn into shreds and thrown into a neighbour's wheelie-bin. Now how did Lisa react when she heard of the winning entry and knew the girl who had stolen her statement? When she asked if her entry had been received, the principal said no; and because no one had seen her place her entry into the submissions box, she had no one to support her claim that she did. Professor Mink didn't know any of the entrants, nation-wide, and couldn't remember if a Miss Lisa…? had entered the competition or not; his only concern was with the statement proffered, not with names.

Miss Drum was outraged and although Lisa did not tell her, until much later that year, that it was her submission that had won, she gave Lisa a book voucher of £50! With this unexpected 'consolation prize money', she bought three unusual texts via Amazon; any reader wishing to know their titles is warmly invited to send a self-addressed stamped envelope to the publishers and you will be told what they are given together with a voucher worth 50% off any future purchase of this delightful story that is seamlessly factual-fictional and totally unique in the history of literature, anywhere. When the International Board of Adjudicators had reduced the winning entries to nine – which is the highest single number – the world's mass media companies decided to televise all proceedings 24/7! And each of the nine *contestants had to sit through interviews televised world-wide. Robyn Banks was one of the chosen nine and was housed in five-star accommodation in Olympic Village. All nine winners, five male, four female, had body-guards, personal valets and butlers and were ordered to wear bullet-proof clothing throughout their stay! As our curious readers will want to know which nine nations made it to the grand finale, here without further ado let them be known: 1) Robyn, from Chorley in NW England, 2) Radha from Delhi, 3) Paula from Sao Paolo, 4) Hisako from Tokyo, 5) Troy from Texas USA, 6) Benjamin from Tel Aviv, 7) Brett from Perth, Australia, 8) Thor from Iceland, 9) Joshua from Zimbabwe, Africa.*

Radha from Delhi was a fourteen-year-old girl who wanted to be a film-star in Bollywood; she loved ancient Indian tales and legends and had begun to write her own novel; she had 'taken' a statement from one of the sacred writings of the Upanishads, but too long to quote here.

Paula from Sao Paolo had based her entry on a sentence taken from The Alchemist, *a novel by Paul Coelho; she was twelve years old and loved cosmology and believed that stars are souls waiting to be reincarnated.*

Fifteen-year-old Hisako from Tokyo submitted a haiku from an ancient text first published in China; her love in life was Taoism and Taoist poetry.

Troy from Texas (USA) was a fourteen-year-old native American Indian who lived on a reservation and submitted a sentence first penned by Sitting Bull *in 1878 and dedicated to the Great Manitou.*

Fifteen-year-old Benjamin from Tel-Aviv submitted a statement taken from Ecclesiastes *(rumour has it that his entry was the panel's second choice) but after meeting Radha, he* decided to 'drop everything and study Sanskrit'!

Brett from Perth, the oldest candidate at sixteen, was brought up in Alice Springs and submitted a sentence taught to him by the local shaman.

Thirteen-year-old Thor from Iceland submitted a sentence urging us all to worship the moon for she 'protects humanity every night'.

The final candidate was fifteen-year-old Joshua from Zimbabwe whose father was a farmer and who worshipped the powers of Nature; his submission asked all men to revere Mother Nature and follow her sacred laws.

The international panel of judges reflected all shades of opinion – informed opinion, let it be said! – and was very thorough in its deliberations. They finally opted for Lisa's magnanimous statement. 'The Supreme Being lives in the hearts of all', and when the other candidates read it, in translation or not, all agreed that it was unquestionably the best statement submitted and one they would take back to their country. All agreed it was a statement that should receive the maximum publicity but, more importantly, was a sentence to memorise and live by! The award ceremony was televised globally and each candidate was asked to comment on the competition and which of the prizes on offer would he or she have chosen. The publishers of this extraordinary text prefer not to say what Robyn took as her prize but she did choose, not one, but three. Many will think that the winner should have been awarded every prize on offer and they would be right; to come up with a statement that is deemed applicable to everyone born on Planet Earth today and for all future generations, deserves no end of praise, honours, presents, medals, awards and shed-loads of adulation.

What must be said is that Lisa seemed unchanged by such a

cruel blow. She went about her business as brisk and as single-minded as ever. I assume she felt pity more than anger and showed courage not to retaliate; she wisely preferred to suffer the deception in silence.

'*Like any musical instrument locked in its case,*' *I said to Miss Drum shortly before I left,* '*Lisa keeps her notes all to herself!*'

The reference to music made her grin like a leprechaun; everyone in the staffroom noticed it because, apparently, she rarely smiled or grinned. I discovered later that she sang in a choir dedicated to church music, the Gregorian chant in particular which she loved with a passion; in the classroom, alas, she was surrounded by students who only wanted to listen to 'pop music' and would turn a deaf ear to anything else. Each of us has a cross to bear and that was hers.

Readers may think that Lisa's entry rightly won the competition and that would be the end of it; what began as a simple school competition soon turned into a global contest and in the fullness of time, ran its course! Or so it seemed! Despite the 'global' acceptance of Lisa's sentence as the prizewinning entry, especially by each and every competitor, things did not stop there. And why not? Well, listen to this! Many leaders (and not only leaders) of world faiths and religions, disagreed with the winning entry and even ridiculed the reasons given by each adjudicator for his or her choice. Many so-called 'god-fearing' individuals found fault with the very theme of the competition, calling it the brainchild of the Anti-Christ! As for atheists, agnostics, sceptics, existentialists, hedonists, nihilists and devil-worshippers, they, too, were up in arms not only at the competition or at the winning statement (which they dismissed as bull-shit!), but also at the list of prizes on offer, calling such the cancerous excesses of capitalism! Their criticisms had deep-reaching repercussions and led to events that no one could have foreseen. And so I include them here because they are important in themselves and are directly related to the competition that Nabi had overseen and certainly add great interest to my diaries. From a previous section that discussed what third millennium readers wanted and needed to read, what now follows is very much in keeping with that requirement. After all, this text is now a novel-in-the-making, and belongs as much to me, Noah Azrael Salmon, as to the eyes of all future readers, the omniscient narrator and to Nabi. That said, the competition, its result and aftermath led to life-changing experiences not only for Lisa, but for countless young people across the globe. Nabi was certainly a visionary, greater proof of which is found in the following chapter.

CHAPTER 13

As mentioned, the competition was severely criticised by non-believers, non-Christians especially, who claimed that the statement 'Love your neighbour as yourself' had failed miserably and so any competition based on it was nothing but a huge farce and waste of time! And so these very disbelievers, critics, even iconoclasts organised their own competition with the question: Why has the statement 'Love your neighbour as yourself' failed, and failed miserably? Nabi appeared to me early after the competition was announced, saying that I should follow it seriously. Just as WW2 was a continuation of WW1, so this counter competition was, in reality, a continuation of the initial one that I had – with his help – brought into being. And just as my local college competition soon turned into a global contest and was followed religiously the world over, the same occurred again, as if another World Olympics! I was very curious; I already knew that many leaders – and as a consequence, their followers, – of world faiths and religions disagreed with the winning entry and even ridiculed the reasons given by each adjudicator for his or her choice. Professors of Theology, Nobel-Prize-winning scientists and authors, eminent statesmen and women, politicians, super-successful businessmen, galactic celebrities of stage, cinema, radio and TV, editors, popular journalists, nihilists, anarchists and... (the list grew by the day) all attacked the competition, claiming that the instruction of 'Love your neighbour as yourself' hadn't worked in two thousand years and so anything based upon it would likewise fail! 'Time is the best teacher', they raved and ranted, making sure that the whole world heard them! And when leading reporters pinpointed areas where war, conflict, oppression, famine, poverty and civil strife were the 'norm', their opinion was widely accepted; it seemed as if mankind was not ready or prepared to accept the New Testament teaching because it had proved a failure since its inception. And so the dissidents, calamitous in their opposition to the competition, came up with one of their own entitled and mentioned above.

And its supporters, although no less rich than the supporters of the original competition, offered paltry prizes, saying that to work out the answer was a 'no-brainer'; after all, evidence for its dismal failure was all around us! And it would be the institution (school or college) that would benefit, not any individual winner; a new laboratory, or library extension, or a new modern language wing or a new gymnasium, whatever the winning institution felt was best for its needs.

And indeed the counter-competition was launched along the same lines but involved every school and college across the globe. In a surprising move, the organisers extended the age-limit to allow undergraduates to enter! They widened the net to include society's brain-power, convinced that nothing could explain the reason for the teaching's failure except that the teaching itself was flawed and totally at odds with basic human nature. The organisers also chose a very different list of 'adjudicators'. They agreed upon a panel of twelve judges that consisted of two retired military personnel (from Afghanistan and Syria), two retired Supreme Court judges (from India and Japan), two high security prison wardens (from the Soviet Union and China), four fully paid up members of the World Humanist's

Association (all four from Europe), one eminent professor of criminology (from Israel) and one prisoner in Death Row (in the USA). News of the list of judges brought immediate disapproval from evangelical churches, fundamentalists, Jehovah Witnesses, Christian Scientists, Seventh Day Baptists, the Salvation Army, Lutherans, Mormons, Wesleyans, Calvinists, Spiritualists and, surprisingly, from millions of Boy Scouts and Girl Guide groups world-wide. But such criticism did nothing to diminish the immense popularity of the competition; in fact, criticism from such diverse 'religious' groups greatly added to the competition's appeal and interest.

All candidates had to submit their submissions within one calendar month. As to be expected, it was faith schools that took up the challenge seriously; but the winning entry came from a tiny primary school in Spain, near Alicante. Their entry read as follows: The statement, 'Love your neighbour as yourself' can only 'fail' if, and when, it's not put into practise!' I can tell you all that, according to the final report of the judges, over 98% of the reasons given in umpteen entries to explain the alleged 'failure' of the 'love your neighbour...' statement related to social conditions, inequalities, injustices, poverty, the class/caste system, man's inherent evil nature and the work of the devil; this last reason was by far the most widespread! Most responses focussed on the evil in the world claiming that 'if man is born a sinner, evil inevitably will result!' Others complained that the statement was 'far too idealistic'; more pessimistic entries claimed that 'because we don't love ourselves, how can we love others?' The panel of judges, although hugely sympathetic towards the competition's theme, were looking, intuitively, for a solution to the undoubted presence of evil in the world. If the 'love your neighbour...' notion had failed, what then would or could succeed? Mankind certainly needed urgent guidance and that was what most adjudicators sought. Totally negative entries were dismissed; the world demanded practical advice. Surprisingly, it took a nine-year-old girl, named Inmaculada, a pious pupil at an unknown primary school to come up with the answer that every single judge accepted unanimously.

Even though the panel of judges fully agreed among themselves that Christ's statement had 'failed', they all acknowledged that it had never really been put into practise nation-wide. Yes, there had been monks, nuns, hermits, the desert fathers, monasteries, religious orders and so on, but apart from such minorities, it had never been seriously practised by majorities. It was reasonable to suppose, therefore, that had it been applied seriously by the majority, it could have worked and could still work today! And do you know that it was the prisoner in Death Row, together with the two retired army generals from Afghanistan and Syria, who had convinced the other judges to opt for little Inmaculada's ever-so-simple submission that was seen as the best solution! Senseless killing and maiming on the battlefields arose from hate, blind rage and misunderstandings, things that humans can avoid by turning the other cheek; prisoners in Death Row (not all!) who often spend years alone with their guilt, have ample time to contemplate the meaning of life and realise that savage behaviour based on loveless actions leads to misery, despair and at worst, to the electric chair. When the results were published, all those who had supported the second competition turned, as if one voice, against the adjudicators and derided their decision and scorned their findings! They felt betrayed and accused the panel of judges of siding with the 'enemy' and were no better than traitors! The panel of worthies who had judged the competition graciously refused all such criticism and said their choice was unanimous and wouldn't be changed! As one astute reporter wrote the next day, 'no Christian love was lost between the two sides'.

I shall say no more of this now, but it will give you readers ample food for thought and discussion. I was later told by Nabi that a competition using the very same caption as on Earth took place up in the celestial antechambers of Heaven. Needless to say, 'the celestial voice' tallied with Inmaculada's; put into practice the famous words of Christ and the world would undoubtedly be a much 'better' place! But it should be mentioned that similar statements taken from sacred Hindu and Buddhist texts also found widespread support in the celestial antechambers. And that is to be expected among the 'star-people' for they all promote what is true, beautiful and good.

Reading this, Casey felt compelled to pause and reflect on what he had just read. Our thoughts, so he told himself, do dictate how we live and a notable example of this would be his own Uncle Noah, especially in his retirement years. He may have become a recluse but by no means was he a moronic drop-out, a social misfit or a couch-potato! He kept herself extremely busy and became, as one teacher-friend of his called it, '*super-busy*', or in today's usage, a 'workaholic'. Casey, on learning this, wondered if he, too, had been super-productive? It seems he was, but Casey knew he would have to wait a little longer before he uncovered the whole fascinating truth about Uncle Noah's novel which some readers may prefer to view as his obituary. Yes, Casey is coming round to the notion that the later diaries may be considered to represent just that but with this significant difference; it was written by Noah himself, and not by another!

From the opening lines of a statement addressed to no one in particular, Casey realised that Noah's life had been a noble but secret mission to find the meaning and purpose of our existence on Earth and once found, to broadcast it to all of mankind. Noah clearly had such a question in mind early on; it is, as he claims, born with us, it forms part and parcel of our individual make-up as human beings. And when he met Sunita and then, dramatically through her, Nabi, that initial question took on a whole new significance. For, indeed, life does have a purpose and a meaning. Nabi leaves no doubt about that but for countless millions, life's purpose means above all else physical well-being, sensual enjoyment, bodily comforts, a de-luxe home, an expensive car, lavish holidays, a film star wife or husband, super-intelligent offspring who religiously follow their parents' footsteps and hope to earn shed-loads of cash to 'invest' in their chosen bank! For such 'lost souls' these desirable things mean heaven; it has to, simply because in their sleep-filled eyes, there is no other. And so when Noah was asked to 'awaken' a dormant humanity sleepwalking its way to decay and death, was he really totally conscious of the task ahead? Probably not. But he had enough to go on; celestial powers stood at his side, he had the lotus-flower talisman and he had received esoteric training in the sacred Mystery schools that hardly anyone seems to know about. Divine help, the lotus-flower and his spiritual 'S.A.S.' training were master tools with which he was to offer his unseen audience real manna from a real Heaven! Away with all 'fake earth-bound heavens' made up of what he mockingly termed 'impermanent snowflake sentiments' based on sense-impressions only.

And Casey willingly agreed, for it was this other heaven that caught his attention for he knew that what Noah was to offer his audience was the very 'Heaven' spoken of in religious writings the world over. Do not philosophers and theologians teach us that we all seek the joy of happiness (the natural fruit of Heaven?) because it's something innate in our being, in our individual psyche? We cannot help ourselves in this; no one sane sets out to end up in misery and pain! Self-interest and personal advantage certainly teach us to seek happiness and that's fine, but how many seek it for *all of eternity* and *beyond*?

Noah did; Sunita was already 'tasting' its reality and Nabi lived in that golden realm and would do so *ad infinitum*! And so, as he read more and more of such 'other-worldly' matter, Casey soon began to be drawn to what Noah offered and what Nabi delivered. For he reasoned so; how many 'men and women of God' can prove to us 'here and now' that such a place, or state of being, exists, or can guarantee its duration for ever and ever? Hardly one; for if they could, the churches, temples, mosques, synagogues and all holy shrines would be full to over-brimming.

At this point in his reflections, Casey has to thank the unseen narrator who has allowed such thoughts to be added to this 'obituary', thoughts that originate in the minds of higher beings but resonate within those who genuinely seek a better world for all of mankind. All such seekers quickly realise that it is our very thoughts and sentiments, whatever their origin or worth, that dictate our lives and help to explain very diverse life-styles and 'levels of achievement'.

And so Casey silently opens his heart to every single reader, asking them all to admire his Uncle Noah who, virtually single-handedly and with a heart that refused to be daunted, took it upon herself to discover, for once and for all, if such a place or state of being (after all what *is H*eaven?) did actually exist! But more than that; for once having established such a place existed (an incredibly difficult undertaking), he then had to grapple with this dilemma; was it also attainable for Tom, Dick and Harry, for Jane,

Jill and Alice?

    Again at this point in his reading of the diaries, Casey felt compelled to take a short break; he needed to reflect on contents that far exceeded the limits of his curiosity and all his expectations. Who among his relatives, friends and colleagues would ever have imagined such a text – a text, let it be said here and now – that may be considered, *inter alia*, as a living voice, but heard from 'the other side'. Casey felt obliged to ask for the reader's admiration because he was becoming increasingly conscious of the enormous task undertaken by someone virtually unknown and yet, also, a relative of his. No one would nominate his Uncle Noah for an OBE or a CBE or even for an illustrious blue plaque to be placed above the doorway of the cottage where he once lived and had his being, or on a wall on the site where he spent his retirement as a recluse. Read on to see why Casey thought that Uncle Noah deserved such an honour. And so without further ado, Casey continued reading Book Eight.

CHAPTER 14

The enormous public interest in the competition reinforced me in my efforts to turn 'half-alive angels' into full-fledged entities. Yet the negative reaction of whole segments of society against the outcome gave me real food for thought. The world, it seemed, was up in arms and so I soon realised that, despite my privileged position as a precursor or teacher of the next stage in human evolution, my undertaking was not without real dangers. It was at this point that Nabi decided to pay me a visit. He was acutely aware of my feelings, doubts perhaps, that besieged me when I saw the ferocious attitude and villainy of millions of people who scorned the competition per se and scorned even more what the international panel of judges had chosen as the prizewinning statement. His presence helped me to no end. Oddly enough, he took great interest, even comfort, from the negative reaction because in it he saw how the initial competition could be continued globally and that had to be a good thing. He also greatly helped me to take stock of my situation, given that now my journals had to be made relevant to my task and to the needs of my readers. In short, what now follows is the advice he gave me; his powers of reasoning always convinced me of his viewpoints that smacked of the wisdom of the ages.

Firstly, as he gently warned me, the journey or quest I was on was very different from what the vast majority on Earth seek and regard as the highest good; they seek wealth, celebrity and sensual pleasures. But at what price? For is it not the case that to attain such things, the mind becomes so distracted that it can't think of anything else? This is especially true of the hunt for sensual pleasure that all too quickly enslaves the mind completely. Those caught up in such a pursuit fervently believe that sensual enjoyment will lead them to that lasting joy sought intuitively by the soul.

Nothing could be further from reality and yet they persist. But how wrong they are! For what ensues is deeply felt dissatisfaction and/or frustration, both of which lead to anger; with anger comes loss of reason and with loss of reason, misery and despair inevitably follow. The frenzied pursuit of wealth and fame is commonly seen as eminently worthwhile; in fact, many consider them 'noble objectives' while others – and these form the majority – praise them as the 'highest good'! Look around you and you'll see that for countless millions, such objectives constitute the ultimate end to which all of human endeavour, everything, in fact, is directed. And unashamedly so. Sadly, it is the pursuit of what I call 'perishables', and not love, that makes the world go round. The rich want more and do everything possible to both protect and increase their wealth; the poor strive to imitate the rich, yet all the while the gap between both groups grows daily. But see the dangers involved. The pursuit of wealth, especially when viewed as the 'highest good', makes the mind its slave. When wealth is sought exclusively for its own sake, life inevitably takes a tumble; the outcome is confusion, negativity and even despair. The great drawback about the pursuit of wealth, in particular, is that, to get it, we very often have to live a lie; in short, we are often forced to live our lives to suit others and in so doing we sacrifice our integrity, independence of spirit and our use of reason. No noble-minded soul would ever be guided by the will or tastes of the 'great unwashed'. Although *well aware of this, I still faced a real dilemma and it took extraordinary boldness and conviction to embark on a quest whose outcome was certainly not guaranteed – despite divine assistance – and in most people's eyes was a no-brainer!*

'How could a simple teacher of math,' they would argue, 'be able to change the mind-set of the masses?' And, of course, they had a point. But I was too aware of the needs of the many to be put off by such incredulity. Just as someone dying from a fatal disease will do everything possible to find a cure, so I, too, would leave no stone unturned to seek a secure and positive outcome simply because therein lay my only hope! My consolation is that some, perhaps many readers will praise me because I chose the latter course of action. I did so because reason told me that the pursuit of pleasures, wealth, fame etc., more often curtail life, not prolong it. History is full of examples of people who have gained possession of such things and yet have been destroyed by them.

How many souls have suffered persecution unto death because of their wealth? And how many have undergone great dangers to acquire treasures only to die in the attempt or have their treasures, once found, stolen? And likewise with those who have perished in order to preserve their 'honour' and how many, probably the majority, who have hastened their death, by reason of excessive sensual pleasures? I had clearly arrived at a turning-point, a metaphorical crossroads; how was I to continue, knowing what I now knew of human nature's weaknesses and proclivities? Desire rules us, whether we like it or not. On the one hand, things looked simple; the unenlightened souls who mistakenly sought happiness in things that are transitory and predestined to perish end up disillusioned and embittered. That, clearly, was not the route to take. Rather, I would strive wholeheartedly to seek that which endured and would guarantee everybody, if that was at all feasible, joy for all of eternity. Nothing but the most resolute of resolutions would be required for me to carry out and complete such a mission; after all, to make a decision is one thing, but to persevere with it to its completion is something quite different. Would I not still be exposed to the thousand and one temptations that thought is prone to, minute by minute? Of course, I would, and I knew it! My mind had to be free of all temptation; otherwise, how else would I be able to devote myself entirely to the quest of attaining the 'lasting good', the bliss that the soul longs for and, according to some eminent theologians and moralists, past and present, already knows? Does not history teach us that the noble-minded follow a different path?

Read the selfless lives of those saintly souls who have tried – and do so to this day – to imitate the life of Christ; see how Buddha turned his back on wealth and luxury to pursue a higher goal which led to his sacred search for enlightenment, the continuous experience of the 'true and lasting good'. Life with Sunita and my meetings with Nabi taught me the wisdom of their choice; I was convinced that the mission to lead mankind to the semi-divine state of 'angelhood', of becoming 'fully alive angels' was the only worthwhile aim to have. For once achieved, the blissful experience of the 'good, beautiful and true' would be ours together, forever. It was an ideal I was drawn to from an early age; throughout my search, I was inspired by the lives and teachings of avatars, both eastern and western. That said, what was I taught in the sacred Mystery schools about the 'good, true and beautiful'? The question is crucial because to answer it, I am compelled to follow Nabi's instruction which was to reveal to all my readers more of what I saw, heard and experienced in the Mystery schools. How else am I to engage and sustain their interest? But much more importantly, how else am I to further my quest and lead the present and all future generations to the next level in human evolution, which is angelhood?

In other words, how am I to entertain readers so that they have no other wish but to read to the very end and crave for a sequel? In brief, I undertook an experiment in the art of living and did so with absolute determination. When in all around me I found a nihilistic devaluation of life, I was consumed with the desire to transmute life's seeming chaos into a meaningful whole. This was no easy task, but I somehow knew I had to become the master of my own destiny, in short, to be master of myself! But to master oneself is the hardest of all possible undertakings.

After due reflection and consideration, I willingly and enthusiastically took up the challenge; what now follows is an authentic account of my struggles and setbacks along a path, although ancient, only five others on the planet were willing to take. To live on the edge is never easy and if it's true that the events of life are divinely willed, then I can honestly say that I have sometimes fought against them! But destiny prevails more than we like to admit. The classical notion expressed so succinctly in the Latin tag, amor fati, *love of one's fate,* is no easy thing to acknowledge, never mind accept; yet the notion tallies very well with the Christian concept of 'Take up thy Cross' and with the Vedic concept of karma; we are who and where we are because of words, thoughts and deeds done in previous lives. What I decide here and now will have consequences, if not tomorrow or next week, then sometime soon, because all our actions, and in particular our conscious actions, lead to results that affect our thinking and our feelings in the future. My decision had been made; to continue with my diaries or memoirs that had to include my sabbatical year in sacred Mystery schools. And for *this to take place, I will have to use the simplest of thought-patterns with the clearest of vocabulary. In this, I am following a favourite sentence of a teacher from Tibet with, for me at least, the rather curious name of Rinpoche Rigden, who always began his 'lessons' with a three minutes' silence followed by these powerful words:* "I don't speak for you to understand me. I speak so that you cannot misunderstand me!"

And so his words will be my guidelines in all that follows. I say this because we all know that whatever is said or written is open to misinterpretations, confusion and misunderstandings. The party trick of 'Chinese Whispers' teaches us the fallacy of dependence on the spoken word. After all, anything, so it seems, can be put into words; furthermore, whether spoken or written, nothing is beyond error or criticism. But because the 'lessons' taught in the Mystery schools are so important for mankind's welfare and future evolution, a major goal of mine, especially in what follows, is clarity of expression: but that highly praiseworthy attribute depends in turn on clarity of thought. That said, what now ensues in this novel based upon my written diaries is placed, openly and unconditionally, before the 'tribunal of scrutiny' made up of every single reader of this text. For each of us on this planet, whether a reader of these diaries or not, yearns to have a life worth living and a future worth having. All my teachers – especially soft-spoken, bright-eyed and seemingly always 'living-in-the-present-moment' Rinpoche Rigden – knew this to lie at the heart of the human condition. We all desire our lives to have value, purpose and meaning. It was he who, one evening after an inspiring lesson on the grand concept of the Wheel of Life, told me to include all my enthusiasms, aspirations and even my assumptions in the novel-to-be so that they become those of my readers, too.

'We are all the same deep-down, you know. Future readers will gradually become aware of that simple truth and so write your text in the spirit of an "investigation" that will allow them to discover what you have discovered, for if they are to make something of themselves, they'll have to take a good look at themselves first. And they'll do that willingly, because most have inquiring and adventuresome minds.'

I can still hear his voice, yes, even now, as I write his words of deep solace in my journal. I knew he was right, so very right. I had been given a treasure-trove of ideas and every single idea was worth thinking about. But I also knew from my classes that all our teachers wanted each of us to re-evaluate our values and re-examine our examination of our priorities; no stone had to be left unturned. And that was a hell of a problem for some of us and it would be no different for my readers. For they, too, would eventually have to start afresh, as it were, so as to join me in living life as an experiment, to see and feel everything anew, to cultivate a 'dangerous curiosity', if I may say as much, as a prerequisite to the search of that undiscovered world that lies in each of us, and which, through Master Rinpoche, I had seen and had been able to recognise as everybody's too. It was our natural, human inheritance, a major jewel of which was living life as 'fully awakened angels' clothed in flesh, and as such, much closer to wearing the crown itself, the state of immortality, the end of the eternal cycle of rebirth and according to every teacher in the Mystery schools, the ultimate goal of human existence.

Wow! What a goal! And it starts for you, each and every one of you, today, here and now, and that's why I was encouraged to tell all readers of the supreme privilege it was (and still is) to be invited to live 'experimentally' and not as automatons, robots or somnambulists. Either we are sheep or shepherds, slaves or masters of our destiny, gods-in-the-making or ragged scarecrows left to rot in barren fields. The choice is ours: more specifically, the choice is yours! No one but you can change your circumstances and options. And so it all boils down to this question: what must be done to wear immortality's crown? What must you do today *to begin to become what so far you are not? You each know the lives you've led that brought you to this point and also how you became the person you are, here and now. But so far – and this you know full well – neither you nor I are free from desires, illness, decay, sorrows, old age and eventual death: in short, Mount Olympus hasn't been reached yet. How am I to blaze a path towards that noble home of the gods so that you can all safely follow? And as I asked myself that very question, it occurred to me that any reader who had got this far would know that I was no longer on Earth. Is it possible that as you read this, I may be looking down on you all from the timeless heights of Olympus itself? And if so, what would I expect to find there? Is it not prudent to have some notion of one's destination, especially one's final destination? Of course, it is; and so what follows has been given as a special dispensation to all readers genuinely interested in the 'final destination', that 'undiscovered country from where', so we are told, 'no traveller returns. And this is where I can introduce another teacher in the Mystery schools called Amida.*

She lovingly taught us how to study ancient civilisations, Egyptian, Chinese, Akkadian, Babylonian and spoke of them as if they were present here and now. She would recite verses taken from Sanskrit and Akkadian and had even learnt several songs in Babylonian that, so she said, were sung to every child when in the womb and, later, when at nursery school and so by the time they had reached primary school, all such 'cradle-songs' had been learnt never to be forgotten. She claimed that all such lullabies had their origin in a place the ancients called 'Pure Land' and that she had visited that blissful realm many times, especially when just a child. Hearing that, I stood up from my chair in the classroom and asked her point-blank if she could tell us a little more about this 'Pure Land', a place I had never heard of ever.

CHAPTER 15

"Of course, Noah! You have been there many times as has every person in this Mystery school. It is the land where you were first 'born' and to where, ultimately, you shall return, intact and whole. In that blessed place, there is no suffering or sense of being separate, no growing old or rebirth, no ignorance of who we really are, no sense of karma. Above all, Pure Land is where there is no desire whatsoever for there we have everything and more. One feature that you'll clearly recall from your visits to that land beyond the sky is that no two days are ever the same. There, of course, days, weeks, months, years, indeed, the very concept of time as we know it on Earth does not exist. But from my various visits (I have relatives there), nothing is ever the same or jaded but is always new, intriguing and full of wonder. Pure Land is built on an indestructible, eternally present living matter known to its residents as 'Pre-Cambria'; for that solid reason, transience is unknown in the home of the immortals. What all humans suffer on Earth; problems, worries, doubts, fears, uncertainties, regrets, the shocks of everyday living that afflict all souls clothed in flesh, are unknown there. Another unforgettable feature of Pure Land is the light that illumines everything and everyone. Such light is best regarded as creation's own mind for it soothes, cleanses, bathes and nourishes: there is nothing like it on Planet Earth and yet it costs nothing. In a word, it is the very opposite of what some philosophers and theologians have called the 'void'. But the void I am referring to here is not the void of nothingness. For it is absolute, far beyond thought or any idea or concept in the world of ideas. Indeed, it isn't an idea at all for it cannot be logically represented; it is something that can only be grasped intuitively. The intuitive understanding of what the 'void' thus means is enlightenment and it is the search and attainment of that 'state of being' that explains your very presence in this school here and now. Never forget that, as you return to the shadowy world of transience and suffering, to teach others the way out, upwards and onwards to 'fully awakened angelhood' which is the highest quest any soul can undertake!"

Heavens! I never thought such a reply possible. But I was unable to forget it and so what I have written here for readers is a faithful record of what Amida said. The whole class was mesmerised. Where else would any of us hear such an account of what I took to be the Heaven of the four gospel writers? I really hope that every reader reads her words at least three times over, slowly and lovingly, for it contains untold truths that need to be heard and remembered. Try this method of reading her words for a week or even a month and reflect on them and see what comes to mind, literally. It is something I still practise. That said, let me now return to what else is in the diary for this period.

I must say I really enjoyed (all her students did) her classes, especially when she sang songs in Babylonian; it's such a musical language. Amida vividly remembered living in one of the temples in the Babylonian era and sometimes would tell us how the ancients lived and thought and how much humanity had 'lost' since those times. More than once, I saw a tear come to her eyes as she spoke of her early life in the temple before becoming a temple dancer in Babylonia. She spoke so movingly about the games and past-times all the children played at school and in school-holidays, all the great festivals that happened on special dates, the equinoxes, total eclipses of the sun, the full-moon in Spring and in Autumn, dedications to the lords of the universe and beyond, the visits of extra-terrestrials in their incredible space-ships that could land on mountain-tops, or enter the sea and whose occupants knew all about the earth's magnetic forces and 'space-portals' so that journeys to earth were a matter of hours, not years. And when she spoke of such things, she radiated such a lightness of being that we all could see a halo spinning a good metre above her head; she once had told us that the 'higher the halo, the greater the spiritual aura' that all teachers in the Mystery schools have and can make manifest at will. She was right because another teacher I met in the second school showed us his halo, too, but more of Kalachakra later. I asked her one day where was all this knowledge that she had and could quote from and draw on at will stored.

"Oh, on clay tablets, of course. All the great teachings are preserved on tablets of clay or stone. Did not Moses write the Ten Commandments on stone? But clay is better and when such tablets are buried in vaults beneath the sand, they can last for millennia. That is why pottery was such a revered profession in Mesopotamia; were not the Dead Sea Scrolls found in pottery storage jars? Indeed, they were; there is a whole world of knowledge stored on clay tablets waiting to be discovered although very recent wars in Iraq and Syria have caused widespread destruction of such tablets. And they will never be replaced. Such destruction is a crime against humanity, present and future. Fortunately for mankind, in our Mystery schools such knowledge has been stored and digitalised; but better than any mechanical storage is humanity's collective consciousness. That is its eternal vault, refuge and home. You'll be shown how to access such knowledge before you leave us. The mission ahead of you demands such access; after all, you have no idea what events and circumstances you will have to face when you leave us. The ideas you will leave us with will cause many to disown you, call you all sorts of horrible names, treat you as a devil in disguise, even attempt to cause you harm."

Her reply hurt me at first. For my intentions were pure; to help my neighbour to 'see the light' should not cause me, the bearer of 'good news', to feel fear and alarm but rather the warmest of welcomes and the deepest of respect. On reflection, I knew she was right; the ideas and concepts we were being taught differed so much from those in the world I had 'left' for a short while that resistance and opposition were inevitable. What to all of us inside the sacred Mystery schools seemed abundantly clear and reasonable would be viewed very differently by our contemporaries outside. Rather, many of our peers and neighbours and even friends would regard such notions (and many did) as perverse, corrupt, life-negating and above all as unrealistic. It was a hard lesson to learn but, having learnt it, I was much better prepared to present my 'case' to the public at large. That said, it was no easy thing to see and feel oneself as an 'enemy of the people', as if an arch-traitor or devil without any disguise. And because she saw our crusade as 'open warfare' against human ignorance, stubbornness, superstition and complacency, she would often repeat in her classes a fact about ancient Greek life that she wanted us all to learn by heart. It ran as follows: 'In early Greek culture, there were only two areas for effective human action: war and speech.'

And whenever she taught us such facts in her classes, she

would urge all of us to reflect on them as eternal 'truths'. 'Time for reflection' as she called it, formed an integral part of her teaching technique, and it worked. We would sit in the lotus position and silently repeat the sentence given; the mind did the rest. For one whole week, we all had to 'reflect' on that very statement and then share our 'findings'. The outcome was never the same; something 'new' always came to mind.

And that something 'new' sufficed to change our viewpoint, our understanding of the 'truth' day after day. And that was useful; firstly, was such a statement really relevant in today's world? Apart from mercenaries, who truly wants to fight in wars? And as for speech who, apart from actors, broadcasters and liars, really cares a fig? We do have speech therapists for those with speech impediments but elocution, as a subject, is almost unknown. We are all too busy with our mobiles and computers to worry about how we sound! It is the written word, our next text message, that seems to count. What we write or see – the world of adverts, for example – that surrounds daily life twenty-four-seven, dominates sense-impressions from womb to tomb. And so this reminder of what had been crucial to ancient Greek culture was something well worth learning from Amida. Every one of us would love to be regarded as an effective human being but how many relate that enviable status to their speech? Not many. And so why is elocution not on every school and college timetable? Not even in our misnamed 'public schools', in which classical Greek and Latin are still taught, is elocution taught or even offered! And so while in the Mystery schools, I asked for tuition in elocution and in all aspects of speech patterns and in the methods once used in the oral tradition used by famous orators. Readers are reminded that excellent written texts on such topics still exist – some, indeed, were revised and reprinted in the *twentieth century – and so those interested in such writings are invited to send an email to the publishers who will gladly reply with a select list of texts to set you on the road to becoming effective human beings! That said, I took the notions of war and speech to a new level.*

Let's look at the concept of war. The acceptance of my mission had made me wage war against the immensely powerful forces of sleep, inertia, complacency and the often-heard statement of 'I can't be bothered!' And where are such forces most potent if not in schools and colleges in which the ever-increasing 'I can't be bothered' brigade will outnumber those who do care, are motivated and want to make something of their lives. The majority belong to the former category and they are to be found not only in schools but also in the workplace, factories, shops, restaurants, offices and in parliament.

Amida helped me to clarify my task; what she taught us of speech I would use in the writing of the novel. What she had to offer as a teacher and lover of history would be added to what Nabi had already taught me about readers' requirements and expectations. Everything to do with the study of rhetoric, the art of eloquence, persuasiveness and delivery as used by the best orators would become my study, too. For Amida, education was about the proper use and study of language per se. The best of teachers were also fully rounded orators whose use of language (in the class or court room and in the public forum) went far beyond being epideictic or passionate; true orators spoke the truth but – and this is noteworthy – knew what they were talking about as well as the level of understanding of their audience. Those who intend to write for readers in the third millennium would wisely follow suit. With all this in mind, I clearly remember one morning sitting down at my desk to continue work on the novel when I *'discovered'* a quotation in Latin that had been put there by someone, but that someone had not been me. I assumed the author was Nabi or Amida; the mysterious addition to my text read as follows: 'vir bonus, dicendi peritus'.

'The good man skilled at speaking' was the translation and not an *'uncommon'* concept among classical writers. I was intrigued but also encouraged; my *'teachers'*, after all these long and eventful intervening years, were still with me, just as they had promised. And then I thought of Sunita. Could she have been the invisible writer of the Latin statement? It was very possible and an apt reminder of my debt to her because since my retirement and my renewed efforts to complete the novel, I had given her little thought! And as I pondered on the love of my early life, I remembered her *'appearances'* to me and her description of what she had *'discovered'* in the after-life, with her new friends in an antechamber of Heaven. I then stopped what I was doing and tried to remember what she had once told me of her *'new'* home. I recall her saying that she had been shown signs and wonders that would have made my hair stand on end and that she'd met other kindred souls who had welcomed her to the next realm, the next etheric plane of existence, that was now her new home in Heaven where they'll all stay until their merit is exhausted and then, inevitably so, they will be reborn! On her *'side'* when we *'pass over'*, as one day we all must, we will find peace, unity and harmony, the like of which does not exist on Planet Earth! She revealed to me that glories would be shown to us that none of us could ever imagine, in a realm where no two days are ever the same, where the principle 'suum cuique' *('to each, his own')*, was the code of conduct, the rule of law, the cornerstone of all their contentment and bliss. Although I hadn't referred before to her mention of the Latin phrase 'suum cuique', it was that very phrase that made me think it was sweet Sunita

who had added to my diary the quote mentioned above.

Although readers know that she fully endorsed my intention of converting my diaries into a modern novel, I omitted saying that she felt convinced that 2020 was the year to offer the reading public a 'novel of ideas' that transcended commonplace genres (fantasy, sci-fi, magic realism, chic-lit, Y/A etc.), something that had to be fundamentally different, especially in the genre of literary fiction, whether based on 'autobiographical' material or not. Given that the text was based on an experiment in living, the novel had to become an experiment in the art of writing!

In fact, Sunita had said a great deal about literature, about its uses and abuses, claiming that literary fiction can tap into any other genre and thus becomes all-embracing; after all, that is precisely what the very best texts do and do so without exceeding the confines of what is possible. Readers want to be entertained while learning something useful about human life. But what encouraged me and even made me chuckle was the revelation that 'on her side' of the veil – that mysterious dividing-line between life and death – the 'living dead' were actually poring over my text. Sunita politely added that very few on Earth took an interest in the matters that interested her so entirely when a living human being. But that hadn't upset her or had made her negative for she 'knew' intuitively that such a rigid mind-set would inevitably change: in fact, she claimed it was changing as we spoke to each other and that the novel-to-be would greatly help to hasten that very much desired change. My task wouldn't be easy but then, when ever had anything worth doing well been easy? She was there to help me understand what I had written so far and, equally as significant, what was yet to follow. For in both parts, the read and the unread, there would be things that would strike the reader as vague, contradictory or even absurd.

I found these latter remarks a little odd because I really believed I knew what I was writing. After all, Nabi was now at my side and I had attended the sacred Mystery schools, not Sunita. That said, in putting uncommon concepts and ideas into words and words into print, misunderstandings can, and do, so easily occur. So any 'outside and freely given assistance' was gratefully received! My would-be readers needed to be offered the best possible text in terms of content, narrative technique and relevance to their world and to their everyday predicaments. Nabi had already schooled me into what the novel had to include in terms of theme, arrangement and presentation of material as well as in the crucial use of language. Moreover, he explained to me what my text would need to embrace in order to both appeal to the reading public and convince unsympathetic marketing experts. From such 'divine' interventions, not only did I draw inspiration and encouragement, but also was 'shown' how to compose a text that would prove beneficial to everybody who read it; at least that was a prime intention. No one was to be left out! The creation of a true-to-life narrative was to be my fundamental aim and objective. I was going to employ all the cunning ruses of fiction to 'tell the truth, the whole... so help me god.' And so, what I have penned is absolutely true; its clear and simple prose style enables the reader to grasp the meaning without any difficulty, even if many of the things mentioned or described seem to exceed the demands of 'real, lived experience' and at times, may even exceed the unbounded laws of fiction itself.

CHAPTER 16

One of the turning-points to all of us who attended the Mystery schools was a question that ran as follows: 'What would be your ideal day? If I gave you, here and now, a magic wand with which you could make your ideal day, a reality, what would it be?'

The teacher who set us this question was called Kalachakra and was well-known as a 'character' for he always wore a crown made of feathers, similar to what the chiefs of North American Native Indian tribes used to wear. He claimed to remember 'several lives' as a plainsman, having lived among tribes in South Dakota, Arkansas, Nebraska and Minnesota. His head-dress was unusually large, each feather measured over fifteen inches and never ever changed; later, I was reminded that the head-dress worn by North American Indian Chiefs represented the size of their individual aura.

His knowledge of life In the Americas dated from some five thousand years before the arrival of Columbus. He would sing to us in the ancient tongues of those long-forgotten tribes and would tell us stories of their amazing feats of survival in the desert regions of Nevada and Arizona, in regions of what is now Canada, in particular of the three so-called prairie provinces of (Saskatchewan, Manitoba and Calgary) and in the highlands of Peru and Mexico. He spoke to us of several lost kingdoms and cities that thrived in the Andes and was especially fond of his years in the lost Peruvian city of Paititi. He claimed that such tribes had 'living contact' with ETs who often visited their capitals in their space-craft and helped them to build their palaces, monuments, temples and lines of communication. His lessons, if repeated in any school, college or even in the most advanced universities in our world would be considered as figments of an imagination fuelled by the strongest hallucinogenic drugs possible! Even some of his awestruck students sometimes doubted his claims that were truly beyond belief, but because he spoke from his own lived experience he always managed to sweep away their initial doubts.

When 'in class' in those Mystery schools, we quickly learned to drop our prejudices and ill-informed opinions about almost everything. For since birth, we had all been exposed to ignorance, superstition, denial, the shifting world of opinion, rumour, bias and to the widespread acceptance of belief systems that no longer served any fit purpose.

I clearly remember the lesson in which Kalachakra proved to us on a screen, via satellite technology, the truth of what he had been teaching; he showed us indisputable evidence of monuments, temples, palaces and settlements that now lie hidden under thick jungle or in the waters of remote lakes; many of such buildings lie not far from today's shorelines and are to be found in every continent. He spoke fondly of the lost city of Atlantis, of portals used by our space brothers and sisters (his words) to enter and exit Planet Earth, he showed us how some of the major pyramids in Egypt were constructed by means of sonar resonance, a technique widely used by so-called ETs. One day, in fact, he took the whole school to a hidden cave in a mountain and by means of sonar resonance moved boulders weighing ten, twenty tons and more, as if made of cardboard! Whole sections of cave were moved and 'guided into place' as if very basic Lego toys! He mentioned that the most famous of ancient sites had their 'alignments or counterparts' in the skies and thus were in harmony with the rotation of the planets. 'The world in which you live,' he always claimed, 'your everyday, physical world, is the product of sound and so all talk about the Big Bang Theory is closer to the mark than you may think!'

One day, Ophelia, a strikingly pretty female fellow student from Ohio, asked him about his name, Kalachakra; did it have any special significance?

And, of course, it did; but he said little about it; instead, he set us the task of discovering its origin, meaning and spiritual significance because, so he teased us, 'it had one'. And so rather than repeat what our class discovered – a treasure trove of meaning – I shall leave the question open and, in this way, invite every reader to do some research into the name that, and this is the only clue to be given, stems from the Sanskrit and is linked to ancient Indian philosophical systems.

He always used visual aids to teach us of the regions he mentioned; he had kept copies of very ancient maps made from papyrus that referred in detail to the places he once lived in and knew very well at that time. *And then, with the aid of the latest maps created via satellite imagery, he would compare both old and new to explain how it was that cities, monuments, lines of transport and communication systems had gradually 'disappeared' from today's landscape; 'disappeared' he would say 'but not totally lost!' And he was right: dense overgrowth, land subsidence, flooding or wars had caused ancient sites to vanish from today's topography but often remained intact, although well hidden, by natural forces and the work of human beings. Mother Earth still holds the answer to so much of what we regard as 'lost' to humanity; such sites, palaces, temples and statues lie hidden or have moved elsewhere like so many treasure ships that sank with all their cargo on board. And so, if we were* to penetrate beneath the earth's surface, what would we find? Firstly, that huge band of tectonic plates that often overlap deep below the earth's surface and give support to vast canyons, to countless labyrinths of ancient caves, to deep (and not so deep) subterranean waterways, lakes and wells. Are we not still uncovering beneath ancient cities such as Jerusalem, Petra, Athens, Alexandria and others' abundant evidence of former civilisations and peoples?

'Old Coca Kala' as we used to call him, knew that none of us had any real idea of life in such regions all that time ago. In his lessons, he always compared his experiences of life in such ancient cultures with the life we had and knew today. And so it was no real surprise that his open competition question related to what he had once experienced. And so we return to his question that was as intriguing as it was unexpected:

'What would be your ideal day? If I gave you, here and now, a magic wand with which you could make your ideal day a reality, what would it be?'

Without a moment's doubt or delay, I saw how this question would be worth asking every pupil and student on Planet Earth. And that was my firm intention until something unexpected happened. My first 'answer' to the question was something Sunita had told me when she appeared to me not long after her cremation, 'My day,' I said, 'would be like no other, just as in Heaven, where no two days are ever the same!'

But that was no answer to Coca Kalachakra. 'But what, then,' he repeated, 'would *you* do on that day?'

And when about to reply, the omniscient narrator stepped into our conversation and says the question should be addressed to every reader of this text!

All readers still vividly remember the open competition to find a statement that could possibly match the Christian teaching of 'Love thy neighbour...' and to what unimaginable consequences that arose from it; in brief, it became a universal phenomenon whose effects still reverberate with us all, especially among the younger generation!

The narrator's unexpected intervention was both welcome and well-timed because it kindly invited every single reader to send in their entries describing what for them would be their ideal day! It was a great idea, a stroke of true genius and there was to be a prize: three signed and beautifully bound copies of the illustrious sequel!

Casey (and he hasn't been forgotten) stopped reading at this point; he did so because he was thinking out a really good answer to the question. He told himself he would like a copy of the 'illustrious' sequel, yet knew that if any reader was 'really dying to know the answer to old Coca Kala's curious but perfectly valid question, then please send to the publishers a self-addressed envelope (SAE) who will send a signed copy of the answer in full.

The offer was both genuine and generous but also annoying because all of us, here and now, want to know the answer to a question of real interest to every living soul. Readers might also like to know the answer that Casey believed was appropriate but publishers are not willing to reveal it. Their only concern is with the best answer given because that alone will satisfy the curious reader and thereby help to 'sell copies' and consolidate interest in the promised sequel. All other suggestions of possible answers fall into the category of the non-viable and so are not mentioned. Casey spent three solid hours every day for two weeks in his attempt to come up with a really acceptable answer but was never able to find a totally satisfactory response. And so he returned to reading Noah's journals. Readers can breathe a sigh of relief for all of us are interested in the journals and not so much in Casey's private thoughts even if we like him as a character and are grateful for the work he has done so far. Clearly, we are in his debt but his major task is to reveal to us Noah's life and work that are truly unique, of exceptional interest and highly relevant to our lives not merely here and now but for all future time as well. Noah continues:

Despite the unseen narrator's intervention, I still believed the question should be set to all young people everywhere.

'Let's have another global competition, Olympic-style,' I said to all my colleagues and to my local educational chiefs.

I also contacted national and international news-agencies with my suggestion. It proved an immediate 'best-seller idea'; international educational agencies across all five continents wanted a piece of the action and so within days, news of the global competition was mentioned on all major international news-desks 'on the hour' all day long! Mega TV stations vied against each other to attract the widest possible audiences and so offered mega-prizes for the winning entries. It was agreed that initially five prizes were to be won, one on each continent followed by an elimination process, dependent on the public vote, to choose one winning answer only. A great deal of debate followed for all candidates wanted to know the list of adjudicators; it was agreed that every winner of the Nobel Prize in the year before the competition should be a judge and after voting among themselves the Nobel Prize winners chose nine of its members to choose the winning five. Readers will want to know the names and nationalities of the five candidates.

Ophelia Shaw from Ohio; Gita Patel from Simla; Xiao Wu Li from Shanghai; Kwa Ibo-Yuruba from Nigeria and Igor Ouspensky from Minsk, the only male finalist. Each of these winners received a 'golden holiday' of their choice with their entire family and also a six-figure publishing contract with major publishing houses who guaranteed each of them 'world-wide sales'. They were each interviewed in London and appeared on the BBC World News programmes for one whole week; each spoke about home-life, school days, aspirations and the contents of their entries. Translations of a synopsis (a maximum of 500 words) of each winning candidate's entry appeared in all major languages and were given freely with local newspapers. All translations and interviews of each finalist were made public and televised on BBC WORLD SERVICES; such transcripts were also published in major newspapers and magazines of each of the nations and continents. In this way, a real public vote could occur.

The adjudicators were aware that Chinese viewers (as voters) far outnumbered those of any other continent and so a 'proportional representation figure' was created by the Nobel Prize winners of math, economics and ethics, and agreed upon by all candidates. The date of the crucial 'public vote' was 31 October; the final result would be given on 5 November in London. But full publication of each of the five winning essays would not be allowed until one year after the official announcement of the winning entry! Each of the major publishing houses world-wide wanted to publish a book that contained all prizewinning essays together with a profile and interview of each candidate. In this way, the finalised text was to be translated into all world languages; it was also agreed that a simplified text for children aged from 5 to 13 should be published and copies sold at cost price only.

The patient publishers of this unique novel have graciously allowed the unseen narrator to include the five winning synopses, claiming that to do so would add to the intrinsic interest to the novel and so would reinforce this novel's prime and only purpose. Each finalist had composed a mini-thesis running to some twenty pages of font 12 type.

An astonishing amount of things can and do occur within twenty-four hours and each candidate made full use of every hour except Gita Patel who claimed that the ideal day had to include 'time for sleep but no more than six hours', thus her entry was six pages less than that of all the other candidates. The judges revealed – and this provoked a huge outcry from the Chinese authorities – that the longest 'essay' was that of Xiao Wu Li whose entry ran to thirty pages simply because, in her view, the ideal day would not include 'sleep' which she described as a 'mini-death'! And although she had made a very valid point, the judges agreed that a period of 'sleep' should be included in the perfect day because sleep was integral to human nature; we are all designed and meant to sleep on a daily basis although in emergencies and in times of crisis that fundamental 'law of life' may be contravened! Other 'faults' in other essays will also come to light, but because it was the public vote that counted, sweet Xiao Wu Li, a seventeen-year-old interior design student, awaited the 'final result' as politely and as stoically as the other finalists.

Furthermore, the publishers of this text, in line with the wishes of the judges, have banned the unseen narrator from naming his choice from the list of winning essayists. Readers must be allowed to make their own selection; the principle of 'fair-play', so characteristic of British diplomacy, must not be undermined. After all, the full text of each winning essay will be published under separate cover and will certainly be 'discussed' in the envisaged sequel. And that will only happen if the publishers are granted permission so to do by the panel of world adjudicators whose decision is final and non-negotiable.

After all, the BBC World News has sole copyright to all published transcripts and translations, but it has wisely left all decisions about translations and publications to the panel of nine Nobel Prize winners. That said, it is generally assumed that such permission will be given, otherwise no major newspaper, international TV company or any member of mass media empires would have supported the competition from the outset. The result, in full, of any competition that is global in scale and meaning and is of the utmost importance – by dint of its unquestioned relevance to humanity – has to be made public for it belongs to mankind as a whole. Would any nation's 'threat' of a nuclear attack on another nation be kept hidden from the public domain? Not at all. For the consequences of such an attack would plunge the whole world into a crisis no one sane and civilised really seeks. But with this novel-in-progress, things are very different. The whole world can't wait to get their hands on such a text for everybody has a natural interest in the question: what would be your perfect day?

What lies in store for the reading public is a real gold mine of ideas, concepts, sentiments and values as expressed by five of the world's youngest, brightest talents alive today. With their awesome insights and fearless enthusiasm, their essays will help to launch mankind into the third millennium. They see possibilities in the human condition that far outweigh many of life's certainties! And as Kwa Ibo-Yoruba tells us all in her exceptional essay: 'death doesn't change us more than life does'.

It can now be revealed that the five essays chosen were written by the five 'souls' mentioned as viable co-workers for Noah on his mission. It must also be said that each of these fortunate five had also attended the sacred Mystery schools, but apart from Gita, not one had attended the schools Noah had attended. That being so, readers will not be surprised to read in their essays, ideas and viewpoints that may at first seem outrageous and so far-fetched that they seem to exceed the infinite bounds of modern fiction. But that said, readers are asked to bear in mind that all summaries of essays given have already been accepted as the world's best and unanimously approved by the top panel of Nobel Prize Winners in 2019!

Readers of this text have already read of a host of apparently 'unreal' events, encounters, explanations and 'other-worldly' influences that must have pushed their patience to the extreme and yet, despite all, they are still with us reading page after incredible page, for we all now know we can put our total trust in Noah's strange and secret journals and in such ethereal beings such as Nabi, Amida, Rinpoche Rigadin and Kalachakra. Those named are all eminent teachers and guides of Noah Azrael Salmon, who, when just a young lad, was distinguished by his 'thoughts, amusements and hobbies and, according to his class teacher 'was not like any other boy in his class'. And, if we remember right, it was that same teacher who, all those years ago, claimed that Noah's interest in 'other-worldly' things set him aside, and that one day, 'people will take note of his achievements' and that – and this is significant – 'Noah himself was well aware of his unusual interests and talents'.

And it is due to those interests and achievements that we all now can enjoy reading, with true insight, what each prize-winning essay offered as its answer to a question that rolls off the tongue as simple as saying A B and C. But there is something else, the knowing of which will inevitably colour our understanding of this unusual novel. And it is this: Nabi has allowed Noah to reveal to each hungry reader of this novel the synopsis of each of the finalists, something no other publisher has achieved; copies of each synopsis exist but no one to date has combined and published all five into one purchasable text in English. And what an advantage that is for us all.

For what Noah can now reveal to us – after all, by means of special telepathic dispensation, he was later to meet all the five prize-winning essayists and so he got to know the overall winner – are intriguing, novel-transforming details about each of his intended co-workers that no other human alive had access to, details that are necessary to have in order to understand the choice of the select panel of judges whose decision was final and irrevocable. Noah has decided to speak firstly about Gita Shakuntala Patel, a brilliant young female student from North India who shared many of Noah's classes. And yet her individual 'background' is far from any run-of-the-mill Indian family living in a well-known hill-station in the foothills of the majestic range of the world famous Himalaya mountains. He lets her tell her own story to us in her own words:

"When I was seven years of age, I had a visit from what I will call an angel! For six nights in a row, this angelic figure appeared to me and we spoke as if we were twin sisters. I never felt afraid, or alarmed or had any thought that it all could have been a dream! The figure appeared in a column of intense blue light that was warm and so, so inviting and told me her name was Hinda and that I'd never be able to forget her because she was my guardian angel. And then she added that she had been sent with a message just for me.

"I can't say how it happened but I do remember going to sleep as normal on every night of the six I saw the angel. And then, on these six special nights and at precisely three p.m. (I know the time because there is a clock on my bedside table and whenever I wake up, I always look at the clock to see the time) I would be awakened by the gentle rattling of rain against the window and then I would hear the even gentler flap of her angel's wings as she flew towards me as I lay on my pillow. I also heard very gentle music in the air around us both, but deep in the background. All that she spoke of I treasure in my mind to this day. She told me many things but after her last visit, I knew that I wanted and would become a Buddhist nun!

"To this day, I don't know how I was able to keep Hinda's amazing visits a secret, but I did, and somehow I feel proud of this but also quite sad because I was brought up to share everything with my family who loved me more than anything else in the world. In India, all children are taught to share everything with their family yet, somehow and against my own desires, I never ever told any other person in my family, at home or in my extended family. It was not an easy thing to do, but I feel sure that Hinda gave me the strength of will to keep our secret a real secret but one that at times I began to doubt! I would like to add that when Hinda spoke, there was a light, very bright, in both her eyes but the light was of Heaven, not of Earth.

"From those visits, I knew that I was somewhat 'different', a person chosen for something unique, perhaps? And my intuition was correct for it was her who told me that one day in the not too distant future I would write an essay that would win an international competition and that my essay together with another four essays, would help to change people's perceptions of life and of life's purpose and meaning and even spoke of the Second Coming! Much more of what I was told is contained in my full essay and so readers will have to wait a little longer to learn what Heavenly Hinda revealed to me when I was just a slip of a girl in snowy Simla! When my parents and siblings heard of my wish to become a nun, a 'wife of Lord Buddha' as my father put it, they fully supported me but also said that I should wait a few more years before committing to such a frugal and toilsome life.

"Of course, up until now I had said nothing to them about my secret trysts with an angel although I certainly planned to do so when the final result of the competition was known. By the time you read this – and what I have written so far of my meetings with an angelic figure I hope have entertained you all but also taught you something because what I have written is absolutely true – I will be living life as a novice nun in a Buddhist 'monastery' in Sri Lanka or in Tibet. Who knows?"

It can be revealed here and now that years later – through telepathy – she told both Casey Roebuck and the unseen author of her secret meetings with an angelic creature named Hinda who spoke to her in Pali and that she understood everything that was said.

Although her essay is based on her meetings with an unnamed angelic being, its central focus is an imaginary conversation she has with Lord Buddha that takes place under the very tree where, allegedly, he attained enlightenment, the state of nirvana! That is the simple gist of her entry, nothing could be simpler, yet its contents need careful reading in order to arrive at a reasonable interpretation of her words. For let no reader forget that her essay was voted the best by the cream of human intelligence and achievement in our own times! A truly amazing feat and the first of its kind, ever. The works of Shakespeare have been translated into major world languages, the paintings of Da

Vinci, Rembrandt, Goya, the music of Mozart, Beethoven and Wagner all belong to the world at large, but fall short of an essay written by a teenager that was voted the best in a truly global-wide competition in the third millennium! Wow!

Her prize-winning essay is based on her extraordinary but unverifiable claim of consecutive visits (at night when supposedly asleep) from a celestial being, her own guardian angel. So is her work pure fiction or faction, fiction based on fact? She claims to tell the absolute truth (as does Noah) and no doubt we can accept her meetings with a celestial being when she was seven years old. But her 'imagined conversations' with the Buddha must belong to fantasy, even if, as she claims, her conversations are actually based on discourses Buddha engaged in with his disciples. In them, Buddha shows Gita how to live 'daily life to the full' so as not to incur any sin! And so for her, the perfect day centres on two aspects; leading life to the full without incurring the slightest stain of sin.' It should be mentioned that Gita, in her star-essay, never defines the term 'sin'. In fact, she doesn't have to because in her discussion of how we should behave (in terms of our speech, our intentions, our thinking, our actions etc.), we are shown how to lead a happy, sane and civilised but sinless life. When news of her essay's contents reached the world's press, it caused a furore even greater than the outcry against the winning entries of the two earlier competitions! And why was that? Read on to discover the reason for such a hullabaloo.

Firstly, major critics of her essay claimed that the prime aim of the competition was to provide details of the perfect day as lived on Planet Earth here and now; thus, they wanted to read and hear of 'things' we all could do that were practical, realistic, down-to-earth and that brought the untold joy and happiness that we all associate with perfection, with what they paraphrased as 'paradise on Earth'. Anything less went against the purpose of what had been set and agreed upon. The whole world wanted to be told how everybody alive could spend 'the perfect day' with their family and friends, their loved ones or if living alone (living alone is a major fact of modern life in big cities in so-called advanced societies), without having to be millionaires or members of the landed gentry, privileged classes or royalty.

Such a day had to be within everybody's grasp; the winning formula, therefore, had to be simple, affordable and achievable as well as ensuring that no harm came to any person, animal, plant or mineral. And that is exactly what Gita had provided because in her perfect or ideal day, no other person or thing is harmed or hurt, not in the slightest. The panel of adjudicators saw that and that is why her essay had been included in the final five. Even if much of her essay is about an imagined day in the known life of the Buddha, what occurs in that day is achievable by everybody because Gita focuses on the reasons and intentions behind actions, and not on the actions themselves. In brief, how often do we think one thing, say another and finally do something totally other? When purity of intention is present, such dichotomy does not manifest! Moreover, how often do we disguise our actions? We offer our arm to an elderly person to cross the road, but our intention is to steal their purse or wallet! Gita fully centred her essay on everyday events done with awareness, being awake, as if being in touch with the divine. And that made her win her continent's prize. For we all know that we can, and most often do, 'sleepwalk' through daily life, as if life were a dream. When I read her essay, I was immediately reminded of my own mission which was to 'awaken in others' the truth and purpose of their existence: angelhood! Having been a student at the ancient Mystery schools, nothing less could be expected.

I can now reveal the basic facts about young Gita Shakuntala Patel. Aged eighteen, she was a student of Sanskrit and Pali at Poona University in Northern India. She came from a family of five (she had two older brothers) and had studied both languages from the age of eight. Both her parents were academics and both taught Sanskrit in New Delhi; Gita's father also taught Pali and had spent several years in Sri Lanka and in Tibet. Both parents were ecstatic at Gita's success and became 'celebrities' overnight. As already mentioned, she had spent one whole year in a sacred Mystery school; she had shared classes with Noah taught by Rinpoche Rigdan and Amida. She had read when very young – and she swears it was in a comic – a sentence she could never forget! The sentence ran as follows; *'All things that are, exist either in themselves or in something else.'* She was aware that she existed and knew categorically that she did not exist in herself; for if she did, she would have the power to recreate herself and in effect, live forever and ever. No; she lived in 'something else' and that was what she also wanted to discover; her mission, in part at least, was integrally tied to her search for her true and eternal identity. And with regard to that 'something else' in which she lived and had her being, was it not part and parcel of the 'true-good' that underpinned, so she came to believe, all of existence, here on Earth and beyond the beyond? And with the unexpected but totally welcome visit of her guardian angel, she was enabled to grasp the full and true meaning of that strange statement that she had come across in a comic and with which no one really could find fault. Its meaning was crystal clear and it was that plain fact that had held the attention of a seven-year-old girl!

In her bedroom, Gita kept a small bronze statue of the Buddha whose eyes are closed to the outer, superficial world of change but inwardly are 'open', observing the endless vastness of the mental world within, the source and origin of our thoughts. The statue served her as a constant reminder of a sacred truth – as the Holy Books of India had taught her – that action arises from thoughts. But where those thoughts come from, their country and place of origin is a question few seem to care about. And yet thoughts dictate our lives day and night, twenty-four seven. That unseen but clearly heard voice in the head is the biggest dictator in our daily lives and yet most seem not to know it or even want to know about it. But Gita was a soul apart. Made from a much finer substance, as if the supreme alchemist, she knew she had to come to terms with that inner voice. She had to learn how to control it and by controlling it, become the master of her actions. There was no middle road: the choice was clear-cut. Either she took charge through willpower or become a slave to the 'unthinking' voice inside her head. Put simply, she was asked to wake up or sleepwalk through life and suffer the consequences. She had been blessed in that she had met the dilemma we all face early in her life. To solve it had become her quest and that quest had defined her life. Noah very quickly saw how he and Gita Patel were kindred souls and shared a vision of life and of mankind's potential that few in general life seem to have.

Casey thoroughly enjoyed reading the synopsis of Gita's essay and looked forward to reading it all. By and by, the utter strangeness of reading about what he once termed 'ghostly visits at midnight' he accepted almost as the norm, even though such an incident had never happened to him or to anyone he'd ever known personally. Of course, in fiction, there are no end of accounts of similar 'ghostly' visits, but then who believes what is told in works of fiction?

Noah next, in his journals, mentions the essay written by Ophelia Shaw from Ohio, whose work had made such a deep impression on the panel of judges in the Americas. Ophelia, allegedly, clearly remembered earlier incarnations as a master potter in ancient Israel long before Christ and later as a consul in ancient Rome. Yet her most vivid recollections belong to her 'two lives' (her words) living in vast caves near rivers. Cave-life was not at all barbaric and savage as often depicted; in fact, she was a cave-artist and drew some of the drawings that have been found in ancient caves, especially in India and in China.

Her current 'Earth parents' both worked for NASA and knew everything that was known of space-craft and of missions to the moon and to other planets. They both claimed to have seen UFOs and had no doubts about their existence; they belonged to that countless band of humans who swear to 'sightings' of UFOs on Earth. Her grandparents had met George Adamsky, and had stayed with him in California and knew all about his meetings with ETs and their space-ships. Her essay, also imaginary, centres on a day in the life of a 'mother-ship captain' who transports personnel, goods and materials between Jupiter, Venus and Mars. But on the day in question, Hesiod, the name of the captain, is transporting teenagers from one colony on Venus to start a new life in a new colony on Jupiter. The essay is, in fact, a series of questions and answers between Hesiod and his teenage passengers who have been invited to create the ideal society in an unoccupied region on Jupiter. It must be mentioned here that the teenagers were more than willing to leave 'home' and emigrate 'for a greater cause'. Their willingness to embark on such a venture mirrors that of a number of humans willing to leave earth and begin a new race, a new life and a new society on the moon or on a planet, Mars or Venus.

At this point, the reader is asking: "Fine, but what has all this to do with the essay question?" Where in her 'prizewinning' essay can we find anything of practical use for 'earthlings' living in the third millennium? What in her essay so far has anything to do with what the competition sought? Any vision of the ideal day had to relate to our life here and now on Planet Earth! So, to talk about 'mother-ships' and their use as transport carriers for a bunch of teenagers who wish to colonise a new region in a distant planet is absurd. End of! And that reaction would be justified if Ophelia had not brought so much newly 'declassified alien files' into her text that prove 1) UFOs exist, 2) mother ships certainly exist and can be as much as fifty miles long, 3) that on such floating cities, life goes on as if on an island and that 4) such ships never crash or falter and have to cater for life from birth to rebirth.

What then emerges from the question-answer conversations is a description of a society that is 'heaven-built', a real-life Utopia in which everybody works for the welfare of the rest. Where everything is shared, even parenthood, and so young people don't find it difficult to up-sticks and leave their societies for the 'greater good' elsewhere. Indeed, Hesiod is actually asked by one of the ambitious new colonists to outline his 'perfect day' and his answer forms the bulk of the essay and after having read it, Noah and Casey both see why it won the 'Americas section' of the global competition. It seems that the panel of judges in the Americas wanted to see ideals mentioned and worked upon in the essay and that is what Miss Shaw provided.

The young Chinese teenager, Xiao Wu Li, from modern day Shanghai, used his astonishing knowledge of ancient Chinese culture and dynasties to compose an essay on one day in the life of Emperor Xianglong who ruled from 1735–1796. During his reign, he championed Tibetan Buddhism and Confucianism, art and calligraphy and the famous Siku Quanshu Encyclopaedia. He bequeathed to China as much as the Great Wall and army of terracotta soldiers. That said, Xiao Wu Li took what he believed were the best achievements of ten famous emperors and combined them into his essay that centred on the remarkable achievements of Emperor Xianglong.

In his essay, he gave particular emphasis to a famous scholar, monk and an intrepid traveller who went to India and brought back some of the greatest writings of Indian philosophy and religious belief. Such writings were immediately translated into classical Chinese – a remarkable feat in itself – and which became the nation's bedrock of culture, ethics, harmonious living and laws. Xiao Wu had actually found a MS of a lengthy discussion between the Chinese scholar-traveller and his tutors in India on the very topic 'What would be the perfect (the word ideal was originally used) day to spend on Earth? Xiao Wu could not believe his good luck and so the bulk of his prizewinning essay centres on that very discussion! His essay is truly brilliant, informative and full of untold love and compassion, qualities that won over the rather stern panel of judges.

Xiao Wu placed the setting of his conversation around a fountain in a lush garden-orchard near what is modern-day Shanghai. Mature fruit trees surround the fountain whose waters stem from an ancient lake that never floods, runs dry or becomes contaminated. Filled with water lilies, the famous lotus flower, the lake has its source 'hidden somewhere in distant mountains'. According to the final panel of judges, no other essay could match the 'poetry' of Xiao Wu's setting and description. But what caught their attention even more was the fact that Xiao Wu used the conversation as an inset piece for the much wider theme of what could be the perfect life of a human being. Hence the contents of the conversations beautifully met the needs of the competition question. In short, Xiao Wu uses the setting of the rich lush gardens fed by a mystical river to frame an imagined conversation between master and pupil. What next follows is a gripping dialogue that examines human conduct. And in order to do this methodically, he examines the purpose of speech between human beings, the importance of our intentions that underlie all our actions and thoughts, our relationship to each other, to ourselves and to our immediate environment (and beyond) and concludes by high-lighting the supreme importance of cultivating the ancient (but often woefully forgotten by humans nowadays) virtue of 'Ahimsa' (harmlessness). Needless to say, it was this ancient oriental principle that prevailed as the quintessence of his description of the perfect or ideal day that men can lead upon Earth, our temporary home (because we are not from earth) for 'three-score years and ten'!

Composed in the style of one of Plato's several dialogues, Xiao Wu's essay will be seen by many as the probable eventual winner, especially as it combines two of the world's oldest empires and civilisations. But Noah (and Casey) say: Hold Fire; each essay is a master-piece in reasoning, presentation and in persuasiveness. Let the panel of Nobel Prize-winners do their job: ours is to read and enjoy the works of five of this world's greatest minds. For let us not forget that each of the five have attended the greatest teaching academies on the planet and the teachers in such are no less than ascended masters, the immortals, those who live in the celestial spheres, our true and only home!

The very strange (strange to many readers who have no

knowledge of ancient lives and customs) but astonishing essay of Kwa Ibo-Yuruba is very different in presentation and in method although the theme is shared: What would be the perfect day on Earth? Kwa's essay is based on an African tribe that had settled and flourished near Lake Chad some seven thousand years ago. This tribe, the Chadic, soon became the dominant nation and ruled a vast area of Central Africa for three thousand years. But what interested Kwa was not the domination of other tribes, or the number of different tribal and national languages or their modes of work (herding, farming, fishing) but in the origin, formation and structure of Lake Chad itself. His interest was justified, given that Lake Chad covers almost eight per cent of the continent!

Chad, indeed, is a vast depression and constitutes the largest inland drainage area in the whole of Africa. His view was this: if a Supreme Being created our world (because nothing is an accident), then what can we learn from, and about, Lake Chad that can teach us something very profound about our Creator? His starting-point was unique; no other candidate had approached the question from such a viewpoint. Kwa accepted totally the belief in a Supreme Being or Cosmic Force that had created everything and that behind this act of creation lay the Creator's wish that everyone born on Earth (and elsewhere in all the galaxies) should lead a happy life. It would be pointless, indeed, impossible, for the Supreme Being Who, allegedly, is all loving, all-knowing and all-perfect to create 'imperfect' creatures so as to torment and plague them with countless problems. How stupid would that be? And so for Kwa, where she was born, the exact physical location, the precise time of physical birth and to whom she was born, the true identity of her parents, were clues in her search for 'true knowledge' of the Creator. And so she studied the region of Chad, Lake Chad, its geology, climatology and its famous drainage system over the ages. Lake Chad, so she soon discovered, is blessed because of the presence of water, a relatively rare asset amid the deserts and vast sand dunes in Central Africa. Its inhabitants necessarily had to learn to live in harmony with Nature and follow her strict laws; to do otherwise would lead to extinction. Aware of this, Kwa asked herself the essay question: what would have been for her ancient ancestors 'the perfect day'? This, after all, has to be answered and the answer, if one is to be given, has to have relevance to present as well as to all future inhabitants of the region.

It was an amazing undertaking for virtually all of her contemporaries said that the region is backward, economically 'poor' and unable to support its current population. The region lacks oil reserves, diamond, gold or coal mines, has relatively little 'strategic' importance and relies on basic industries of farming, fishing and herding that serve the local populations only. But in times of drought, famine, natural disasters and pestilence, nothing can be done and so millions just suffer: families, livestock, crops and fish reserves. The threat of desertification is ever-present; in other similar regions 'tourism (safaris, etc.) give a welcome boost to local economies, but not in Lake Chad. That said, is the region God's only mistake?

No, claims Kwa, because God, by definition, can't make mistakes. Moreover, there are many areas of the world that are, arguably, worse off! War-zones in Iraq, Syria, Somalia, Sudan, Afghanistan, Kurdistan to name a few are clearly worse off. And the blame for such 'disaster zones' is not the Creator's but mankind's; human greed, folly, ambition and depravity. But let's return to the Chadic tribe; we know it prevailed in the Lake Chad region for over three thousand years. But how and why? For, let us repeat, as she repeats: nothing is an accident. And so Kwa looked further into this tribe (one of her direct ancestral tribes) to see if she could find clues, reasons, methodologies that would provide a solid basis for a convincing essay answer. Now, the fact that her essay won her continent's prize has already told us that she must have unearthed astonishing 'facts' and 'figures' that bowled over the panel of judges. But how? Noah can now reveal that when Kwa was in one of two sacred Mystery schools in Nineveh, she met a teacher named Buhosodan who had lived in the Chad region some five thousand years ago. His brilliant 'lectures' or 'talks' of the way of life led in that region overwhelmed Kwa; listening to him, she immediately felt she was put in touch with her 'soul' (her words) and simply wanted to learn as much as humanly possible about Chad life: its languages, customs, festivals, traditions, modes of wear and of worship, its foods and relationship towards the environment. Buhosodan, like all the teachers in such Mystery schools, knew 'everything and more' about his subject. Kwa asked to become Buhosodan's student but was gently refused, not for any negative reason, however. The policy in such schools is that all students attend every lesson offered, fulfil all class assignments and learn from every teacher as well as from all fellow-students.

Buhosodan kindly promised Kwa to be always 'accessible' to her via telepathy and that is what happened. Unknown at the time to Kwa was the significant fact that Buhosodan was a close friend and relative of Amida! But more of that surprising piece of news later. Kwa was able to draw on Buhosodan's vast and unparalleled knowledge of the region; by virtue of such, she was able to show the judges how the 'perfect day' may be spent, and enjoyed *'now'*, but not only in Chad, but across the globe. So what then, in a nutshell, did Kwa write in her essay that can benefit us, the current readers of this strange, getting ever stranger, novel? This is what we all want to know and want to know now, right?

Kwa was very fortunate because Buhosodan had kept a diary of his 'time' in the region and had copied down 'living conversations' between the locals. You may wonder how could it be that anyone living in Central Africa some three to four thousand years ago would keep a journal? It sounds farfetched because the Chad Basin is a long way from Babylonia, Ancient Greece and India where, indeed, 'written' records do date from those times. But Lake Chad? When we learn that Buhosodan had been sent from another galaxy to help the locals to lead meaningful and happy lives, it sounds less preposterous. He naturally brought advanced technological tools with him that the locals used in farming, fishing and in herding. They were taught that the world is a living organism that has to be protected, nurtured and studied because it has its own laws of do's and don'ts, which, if heeded to, provide all that man needs on Earth for fulfilment, evolution and understanding. Buhosodan became a local 'wise man' and was as much revered as any sage in ancient India. In an aside, he once told Kwa he lived over five hundred years but moved around the region so as not to arouse suspicion. In all, he lived over one thousand years as a teacher and chieftain in the Chad region.

In short, Buhosodan taught his 'people' how to live in their environment and how to behave towards each other for 'we are all the same and come from one source'. They observed the changing seasons, knew when and how to plant crops and how to care for their animals and materials. Kwa's essay centres on one day in the life of a farmer who follows Buhosodan's advice to the letter and performs all his actions as if he were a monk in a monastery. In short, *'Everything done was performed as an offering to the Cosmic Being.'* This simple practice explains why Kwa's essay was so successful. Its source is in a concept Buhosodan taught his fellow tribesman and which they 'practised' daily. They were taught from childhood to care for each other and to treat everything as 'sacred'. Such care 'for and in the community' proved the best antidote against the selfish 'I'm all right, Jack', 'I can't be bothered, don't tell me what to do!' attitudes that prevail almost everywhere today. What comes to mind reading Kwa's essay is the ancient concept of the 'extended family'. No one is excluded, no one is seen as inferior or superior, for whatever lives 'is full of the Lord'. Although unwritten, and probably unspoken, this basic living truth characterised life in the Chad region and was something the panel of judges latched onto in Kwa's essay.

Buhosodan, in a surprising behind-the-scenes remark, informs us that the locals would often ask him about spirits, souls ghosts, metempsychosis and 'apparitions'. This was to be expected because parents, friends and neighbours invariably die and some were very young. He made a point of telling Kwa that he would usually begin answering such questions by saying that 'ghosts are perceptible to the senses, but souls are perceptible only to reason'. Yes, we all have ancestors, we all come from the family tree, we all should respect the dead but we can't change anyone's past, their karma, or their intentions when they were living. Even fundamental issues such as who is responsible for the universe?, What, if anything, 'moves on' with us when we die?, What really can we know? are all questions that humans find important. But that said, Buhosodan would always tell his audience that the world is full of questions, puzzles, enigmas and mysteries, but fundamentally they have no real value. And then he would clinch his argument with this statement: 'All that matters is to understand that we are responsible for ourselves, our thoughts, words and actions'.

And it was this pragmatic approach to life's underlying problems that underpinned Kwa's description of the 'perfect day' as led by her forefathers thousands of years ago, but still so valid today. And that's the point. We may refer to the ancient past but such a reference must be made relevant to the here and now.

Furthermore, when the local tribesmen asked Buhodosan such a thing as, 'Does x exist?', he would reply, 'Can we experience x? If not, the question is irrelevant.' The panel of judges quickly saw how Buhodosan's living concepts transformed life in the Lake Chad region and how the Chadic tribe could reign peacefully for three millennia. They lived in harmony with the strict demands of their location and climate and tended the earth as if their own child.

Relations between tribes (and there were several) were governed by the principle of individual responsibility – in brief, you could not put blame for anything on another, and certainly not on God – and on the concept of stewardship: the locals cared for their crops, animals and environment as if honoured guests in a royal house-hold. Buhosodan one day showed Kwa photos of ancient tribesmen walking in a 'sacred manner', forever mindful of their 'tenancy'. Such photos were taken over two thousand years ago, but Kwa's teachers had access to technology not yet available on Earth. In fact, Kwa was given six such photos and she attached 'copies' of two of them to her essay but gave no idea of the real date they were taken. It was clear to all who read her essay of the 'enlightened' state of her ancestors so long ago; enlightened in the sense, they saw 'things as they were', not as they hoped or prayed they would be.

In their final report, the examiners commended Kwa for her 'outstanding original work'; no other candidate from Africa had followed a similar scheme of study. In fact, far too many candidates, so ran their criticism, had eulogised the pampering of the senses as the essential to any perfect day. Exquisite wines, the finest foods, the most exotic of locations all depend on obscene amounts of cash. And so that excludes ninety per cent of humanity. There was no way that such an essay could win a prize that was to be offered and made accessible to the rest of humanity. Such essayists, many the offspring of well-known politicians and celebrities, had lost real sight of the competition's purpose. The head of the African panel of judges held high hopes that Kwa's essay would be the overall winner. And needless to say, so did Kwa.

Now, what has not been said so far is that Lake Chad used to be 'home' to USOs *(Unidentified Submerged Objects)*. And it was Buhosodan who also oversaw all such landings and departures. The modern Chad Basin region spans eight nations; how was it possible for such a 'backward area' to not only survive, but thrive? The answer lies in the optimum use of technology offered to the locals by the 'star-people.' One often overlooked virtue of which is this: nothing was wasted. Modern notions of recycling, ecology, the needs of the 'local' environment, husbandry and crop production, although very welcome and support-worthy, fall very short of what Kwa's ancestors accomplished two thousand years before Christ.

'Waste not, want not' is a proverb in the UK, but its true origin lies in the skies: our space brothers and sisters do not waste. And that ever-so-simple principle of living was taught by Buhosodan to 'his' people in Africa. Very recent history shows us that Africa is now home to famine, drought, disease, poverty, natural disasters causing millions to suffer malnutrition, misery, homelessness, disease and civil strife. What is sorely needed is a rediscovery of the principles unearthed by Kwa in her essay: a new moral rearmament crusade is needed to restore harmony and sanity to so many African states and nations. That need was voiced by Kwa and concluded her essay.

Casey noticed that Kwa added nothing more about the startling fact that Lake Chad was 'once' the site for USOs. The judges obviously made a note of the revelation but did not need to learn more or they would have said so in their final report. But that may not be the reaction of the Nobel Prize judges chosen to decide the overall winner. And Casey is sure that readers of Noah's journals would love to learn more. In today's world, USOs are 'accepted'; sites off California, the Gulf of Mexico, off southern Spain and off the Pacific Rim have all seen USO activity. To open-minded readers, it would be no surprise to hear of such sites, given that the technology used by our space brothers and sisters surpasses ours by light-years, literally. Ufologists will also claim that UFOs are sometimes seen entering and exiting active volcanoes; their knowledge of the elements, metals, gases, chemicals and of their combinations allow them to build craft that can comfortably endure temperatures, speeds, and climatic conditions found on Earth. But that is where we have to leave it. Kwa's essay now gives way to the essay written by the only male candidate in the final five, that of seventeen-year-old Igor Ouspensky from Arkhangelsk.

Igor's parents were renowned physicists who had a passion for New Age Philosophy. Igor had a younger sister, Anastasia, who loved and had a unique talent for abstract art and, at sixteen, won a scholarship to study art in St Petersburg. She loved art and Igor loved fossils; both parents were delighted that they had produced offspring who knew (and were unusually good at) what they wanted to do with their lives. What then had Igor written in his essay that had so impressed the panel of judges?

When very young, Igor showed an unusual interest in 'old bones', but what his parents and teachers more correctly called 'fossils', especially of dinosaurs, and when on holiday in remote regions of Russia would sometimes 'discover' what he called 'biblical bones'. His parents encouraged his passion and believed that one day he would study palaeontology. He also loved minerals and when, in his final year in school, he expressed a wish to study mineralogy, no one was surprised. But that was also the year he wrote his essay that took everyone by surprise, because it hardly mentioned fossils or minerals.

Simply put, Igor loved fossils of such things as dinosaurs because fossils proved they had lived; likewise, minerals, he would argue, were a sort of fossil in that, to create them, processes lasting millions of years had to occur. And because minerals were composed of inorganic substances and had a distinct chemical composition together, usually, with a crystalline structure, his brain somehow connected with them and he made incredible progress with his studies. What fascinated Igor with fossils was the fact that they once existed (their remains prove that), but now are no more. How can that be? How can the mysterious element called Life create a species and then allow it to die off? Yet, with minerals we have substances and structures that have been around for aeons of years but have survived. How and why? In short, Man is a species, a life-form that has evolved (Igor believed totally in Darwin's evolution of man) to the present level of 'homo sapiens'. But the question remains: is it at all possible that Man as a species is doomed to extinction and thus suffer the fate of the dinosaurs? Whether he would admit it or not, Igor was motivated by fear, fear of extinction, oblivion, the Void of the Abyss. And so in his essay, he was also secretly addressing a deep-seated fear of his since early childhood.

Now the source of his fear was unknown to him; apparently, he had been born with it, it belonged to his DNA. That fear became an open wound and soon began to tear away at his resilience. It left him with a 'living' question: was there a solution to prevent the extinction of Man? Igor pondered on this question long and hard and came up with an idea, a belief that won the opinion of the panel of judges. According to Igor's new theory, man would have to live in such a manner that extinction could never be an option. Earthlings would have to behave in such a way that, without them, all the other planets that have 'life-beings' on them in the solar system would necessarily perish. From his parents, Igor had assimilated the notion that every planet in our solar system has life on it, call it ET if you wish, and all depend on each other. The image of the planets rotating around Mother Earth in an amazingly measured way had to be more than what it was.

There had to be a greater significance to that fact. A pre-established harmony among the planets had to exist and it persisted because nothing was done to change or alter it in the slightest. But on Earth, we have had wars, civil strife, persecutions, revolutions, cruelty and social injustices that have upset the planet's 'inner balance'. If mankind continues to do the same things, the planet will implode and fall away from our solar system. For a mind so young to have come up with this question impressed all his teachers at his college in Arkhangelsk; even his fellow students were full of admiration. But another question bothered him even more, but this question he didn't voice until when at one of the Mystery schools: 'What is the cause of human sorrow and suffering? It seems to be endless.' Yet, before he wrote his prize-winning essay, both questions filled Igor's mind.

The young Russian boy soon came to the view that nothing but 'proper human behaviour' on Earth would be the key to its and our survival. In a nutshell, 'How could the routines of the average day in the life of an "ordinary individual" create the conditions for the perfect day while also guaranteeing the lasting survival of our planet?'

It was this question that Igor tackled in his essay. If our Creator loved us as much as we are all told is the case, what would happen if were to try and love our Creator as much as we love ourselves? And in his parents' library, he found 'strange and curious texts' (his exact words) that addressed that very same dilemma. And so he read volume after volume on subjects few in his school, or neighbourhood, had ever heard about. And then when he was chosen to attend two Mystery schools 'somewhere in Asia', he knew, instinctively that he would find answers to his fears and worries. It should have been mentioned earlier that all five students sent to the sacred Schools, did so in their gap year. It was a simple way of avoiding suspicion; travel is what gap-students do, usually travel for educational purposes. Was there any better way to pass a gap-year than in mankind's oldest, yet most advanced schools on Planet Earth? Ask Gita, Ophelia, Xiao Wu, Kwa and Igor, not me.

Igor also learnt how to write a prizewinning essay. He was repeatedly told that to win any essay competition, one had to answer the essay question. "But isn't that obvious, Miss Amida?" he one day asked in class.

"You may think it's obvious, Igor, and it should be, but let me tell you over seventy per cent of essays written world-wide fail because the question posed is not addressed. Students clearly have the knowledge they need to answer the questions set in school and state exams. Most students have done their course assignments, homework quotas and the rest, but somehow fail to achieve. They simply answer their own questions and write what they want the examiners to read. So, we alert all of our students to read, and re-read the question set, at least four times, slowly. We know the clock is ticking and that you may have another important exam that very afternoon or the next morning, but the principle remains: read the exam-question four times and work out what it is looking for as the best answer."

One of Igor's tutors was Akon who said he came from Mercury and was a self-declared 'interplanetary citizen' and had spent the last three hundred years 'on Earth'. Akon was some seven feet tall, had clear blue eyes and had a full head of hair. Despite his having lived on Planet Earth some 'three hundred years', he looked incredibly young, no older than any healthy male adult young in his mid-thirties. When asked how he retained his youthful look, he replied with one word: 'Diet'. He went on to claim that a certain concoction of star-dust, sun-rise dew and an unknown substance found only on the moon was the most favourite of all intergalactic foods and was especially beneficial to children who lacked certain vitamins. The name of such a concoction was 'moon-flower cake' and was eaten by the ton-load throughout the solar system and well beyond. Apparently, OAPs in Jupiter, Uranus and on Venus are given free monthly rations and doubly so at Christmas. OAPs on such planets live well beyond one thousand.

Igor accepted that our intergalactic friends knew of ways and means to 'hide' their true physical age. Coincidentally, Akon's highly popular course in the first school Igor attended was called 'Transcendental Living', subtitled 'How to Live One Thousand

Years on Earth'. Igor literally ran to his classes. What then was young Igor taught?

Akon introduced them all to concepts of harmony, equanimity, balance, measure, posture and rhythm. But wait for it. All of it through the medium of dance.

Wow! And what a spectacle because he taught them dances indigenous to Mercury and to Venus but always concluded with the 'dance of the planets'. Not only was it fun and great physical exercise but through dance, all the students learned how to perform 'as if in the presence of their Creator'. Akon's knowledge of astronomy was boundless; when he taught them the dance of the planets, he always had a model of the solar system before them with each planet's satellites; few students could believe Saturn has eighteen, Saturn sixteen, Uranus fifteen such satellites, whereas poor little Earth has one, the moon. It goes without saying that the experiences had by all students at such schools were extraordinary; they had the best teachers teaching the most relevant of subjects to young people who would oversee the next stage in the necessary evolution of mankind, as a species.

The eternal laws of cause and effect, the principles of karma (that we are 'heirs of our own actions'), the concept of causality (that things are causally determined and not the result of randomness), the law of opportunity and so on. This last was emphasised because what each had been given was the 'opportunity of a lifetime' to evolve and help others evolve. Igor and his class of kindred souls knew how fortunate they had been and so never wasted one second of their time when under instruction. They also knew that they were being offered real knowledge of 'things as-they-are', and not airy-fairy, pie-in-the-sky theories about what they should or ought to be. When they were taught that what we experience, whatever it may be, is a process, nothing more, they felt intrigued; in fact, some felt upbeat, especially Igor. 'It's a universal fact. Everything in our lives is a process or the result of a process.'

Akon was quite firm in his reply, but his reply led to an amazing chain of discoveries for every student. Suddenly, they each knew that the five sense-organs, together with the mind, seen as the sixth sense organ, do not so much define us as to show us how we work as individuals. We are, in brief, a set of processes and so is everything around us. Igor accepted this and decided to study his 'people' and their situation from that viewpoint. And so, the perfect day for 'his people' today is based on intention; how everyone has to work for the common good, following commonly held goals based on a real understanding of karma that Igor described as the 'moral law of the universe'. Self-sufficiency was the aim of their endeavours: waste was seen as crime against both humanity and planet. And they succeeded. From his studies, Igor came across a question that a local woodsman and trapper based in Murmansk had asked Akon two thousand years ago: was there one thing humans could do that would accomplish the ends both of this world *and* the next?

Wow! What a blunt question from a simple woodsman! Akon's reply was equally as direct: "Diligence. Mindfulness. Awareness." And these three words became the lynchpin of Igor's essay. No day lived without one such quality could ever be said to be 'perfect'. And that was the practical advice, openly accessible to everybody alive, that swung Igor's essay in his favour.

And now we come to the declaration of the overall winner. To be sure, all five were winners and pampered as such in their own regions. But it was Kwa Ibo-Yoruba's essay that was finally chosen as the outright winner, world-champion essayist. Of course, there were dissidents. Very many neutrals claimed that Ophelia's essay was by far the best; others, equally as vociferous, claimed that Xiao Wu Li's essay showed 'depths of insight and understanding' unmatched by his opponents and therefore should be declared the winner. There were scenes of protest in both India and Pakistan at the result; both nations claimed that nothing came near the essay written by Gita Patel. Yet, the public vote stood and was fully endorsed by the panel of Nobel Prize winners.

Local, national and international newspapers sold more copies than ever before! Each of the five finalists were asked their views of the final result, but not one disagreed with the outcome. Indeed, the four 'losers' claimed that the questions Kwa raised in her essay were relevant to all of us here and now as well as to all those yet to be born. But better than such profound questions were the facts and figures she had 'unearthed' in her research. Her account of Buhosodan captivated the hearts and minds of all audiences everywhere. Many had heard of UFOs, but very few had heard of USOs. And then throw into the mix the notion that, according to Buhosodan, each of us is responsible for our actions, nobody else. So no one can really blame their parents, their star-signs, their circumstances or their Creator for their predicament, for we are all 'heirs of our deeds', end of. It goes without saying that not one of the five finalists 'breathed a word' of how they really spent their gap-year. Other things were on their minds. Joined together by their time spent in the Mystery schools, the celestial powers ensured they met and formed a new society that will be revealed in the sequel.

They were commissioned to carry the banner forward and continue Noah's exemplary work into the twenty-first century AD. But first they had to wait until the book containing all five prizewinning essays saw daylight; sales broke all records. And once Joe Public had digested the contents, it was inevitable that another outbreak of dissidence and protest occurred, attacking the overall choice of winner. A gallop poll was taken, globally, said the sponsors, and two winners emerged, both sharing similar votes; Xiao Wu Li and Igor Ouspensky. According to the neutral gallop poll, Kwa's essay finished stone last! That said, nothing was to change the initial result. Inevitably, public attention soon centred itself on the 'Fabulous Five' as the paparazzi cloned them. What would they next do with their lives? Each of the five was invited to live international debates in which members of the audience were able to ask any question whatsoever. The outcome of such debates was the same; each of the five would continue to study and serve the needs of humanity.

And that is precisely what they did. But to discover more, all readers will have to await the sequel that is already a 'work in progress'. Their efforts, both individual and collective, are perhaps even more astonishing and unexpected than what has been told so far. Casey is as keen as anyone to read further. He believes that a number of important threads need to be tied up, the least of which is whether the authorities should place a plaque above the front entrance to Noah's quaint cottage not far from Brecon Beacons.

Casey is well aware that the locals, especially ex-solicitor and former mayor, Hugh Dyfed Thomas, have lots of questions to ask about Noah, the real Noah Salmon, who lived as a recluse in their hamlet and never truly got to know him. These and very many other queries will be addressed in the sequel that should appear in 2023/4, the year of the Water Rabbit and, in the Chinese calendar, the fourth of the twelve zodiac signs. Readers are urged to find out more about the Water Rabbit that is considered the luckiest of all the zodiac signs in the Chinese calendar, a fact that adds to the mystery of the secret journals that Casey has had published alongside the five-prizewinning essays written by very close associates of Noah.

His successors have secretly vowed to continue his Herculean work for the present and all future generations born on Planet Earth. Their undertakings, tasks, projects and intentions will lead to a host of unexpected consequences and spin-offs. Did not Noah's simple idea of a school competition seeking a new formula for living also lead to a series of unforeseen events and outcomes? Yes, it did, but such turning-points are integral to the narrative technique followed by the various authors – voices? – of the text and serve to engage reader interest and participation from page one.

Totally disregarding the norms of the novel's *denouement,* Noah had written a poem that he considered fit to either open the novel or close it. According to Ophelia and Igor, journal-keeper Noah actually asked for their opinion and all agreed it should close the text. And why? Because the poem, written in free verse, leaves as many questions as it does resolutions. Full of intrigue based on the mysterious workings of individual karma, the poem leaves the reader in suspense: what will happen next to Casey, Gita, Kwa, the reader? What cards will fall their way this time around, in this embodiment? Perhaps, you will find possible answers in the sequel.

THE CARD PLAYERS (34)

Our days, a deck of cards played out from birth,
an ace, a jack, a joker or a king?

The silent dealer serves each card face-down,
in full accord with what is deemed fair play;

until each hand is dealt, no one dare look
at figures falling seemingly by fate:

with eyes more fixed than any lover's gaze,
mute players scan the cards that drop their way.

One glance, no more, to weigh the pros and cons,
a royal flush, two pairs, or one full house?

Adept at reading body-language signs;
surprise, dismay, elation or regrets.

Their poker face conceals the state of play,
for what is unexpected happens most.

And yet, they play their cards as if they knew
the hidden workings of the laws of life

that operate despite pure logic's will,
for nothing in this world can break the chain

of cause and effect, the yin and the yang,
eternal as the ebb and flow of tides

more constant than the stars that shield the sky
held tight within the morning mind of God.

That's how it is, that's life, and change it won't,
until we learn that karma is at work:

unseen, unknown, unfelt, until in time,
the truth must out, for actions leave their seeds

and germinate, both good and bad; a rose,
or daffodil, sweet orchids or foul weeds

for consequences stem from what we do,
but who knows where, with whom, or for how long?

We bear the cross made up of deeds long 'dead',
performed in former lives in foreign lands.

Our days, a deck of cards served out face-down,
an ace, a jack, a joker or a king?